Steamy BDSM Short Stories Volume 3

PRIMAL, ROUGH, SENSUAL, DADDY DOM, SUBMISSIVE, DOMINATION, STEAMY, ROMANCE, EROTIC

BLAIRE LITTLE

Copyright © 2025 by Blaire Little

All rights reserved

No part of this ebook may be reproduced, scanned, or distributed in any printed or electronic form without express written permission from the publisher. The scanning, uploading, and distribution of this book via the internet or any other means without the permission of the publisher is illegal and punishable by law. Please do not participate in or encourage piracy of copyrighted materials in violation of the author's rights. Purchase only authorized editions.

Steamy BDSM Short Stories Volume 3 is a work of fiction. Names, characters, places and incidents are the product of the author's imagination or are used fictitiously. Any resemblance to actual persons, living or dead, events, or locales is entirely coincidental.

Published in South Africa by Blaire Little

Welcome

Welcome to my salacious thoughts where you'll find bite-sized stories to whet your appetite in more ways than one. Some stories are happy, some are filled with raw emotion, others are rough, others more exciting, and all of them will find their way under your skin.

I love writing spicy romance fiction featuring BDSM elements; I want to get your blood pumping and wanting more!

Come join me and let's explore our deepest and sexiest desires together...

An Experience To Remember...

RYAN & NADINE

> I might hurt you.

I blinked at the screen. The four words stared back at me as my mind processed his words; *"I might hurt you"* - words I knew to be true. He could hurt me. I didn't want to believe it because he came across as this warm and gentle person who himself had been badly hurt by his ex. His words were filled with kindness, but there was also pain and suffering hidden between the letters.

Dating in my forties was hard. There weren't only single men in the sea, but married men disguised as single, which clouded the already muddy and shark-infested waters. There were men collecting women for their harem. Polyamorous men looking for someone extra to join the group. Men who wanted 'one-night stands', 'friends with benefits', 'situationship', and everything in between except an actual relationship. Then there was me, a single female going through some changes and in search of a hot-blooded male who also wanted a monogamous relationship. It was difficult navigating this sea when my life jacket had a hole in it, and I was swallowing sea water.

I sighed.

I missed being touched by a man. Have his hands cup my breasts and feel my curves. The feel of his body brushing up against mine. The weight of him on me as he thrusted inside of me. His warm mouth on mine. His eyes filled with desire. I wanted nothing more than to find my favorite person, but I also wanted someone who could do all those things to me **now**. Someone who released the frustrated tension within me. Someone I could trust not to hurt me physically and mentally.

My problem was my emotions; I was full of them. I was a delicate, sensitive baby girl who took everything to heart. And that meant I could develop feelings for this person helping me release the knots winding me tightly.

I glanced at the screen again, at his words; words I wasn't expecting, but knew to be true. It told me he cared enough to write them and that he didn't want to hurt me. That if we did this, and I developed feelings for him, that we ended it to avoid both of us going through any kind of heartache again.

> I believe you...

I wrote, understanding fully what he was trying to convey. I'd get hurt if my feelings developed into something greater. The lines between my eyes deepened.

Could life please just give me some good news for once?

I had enough 'character', and sincerely didn't think I needed to go through any more crap to build more 'character'.

I'd love nothing more than to receive a message from my *favorite person*. He already knew what I needed and wanted and just magically did everything right because it came naturally to him. Because it was something he wanted to do; to protect and take care of me. And then he'd tell me what I needed to do to please him. I could be his *princess during the day and his slut at night*. I'd love to please him that way. But no, my favorite person was on a tortoise lost somewhere, too stubborn to ask for directions.

I sighed again. My deep breathing didn't seem to help much.

We all had scars. We all had scar tissue rubbing raw against our flesh, reminding us that we're human and life liked to fuck us in the ass without lube every now and then.

We all experienced heartache, narcissistic behavior, and cheating. That's what living meant; we left our house and explored the outside world. It would surprise me if anyone had experienced nothing like that; it also meant they weren't living life to the fullest.

We had to protect what remained of our hearts. Some built walls, others put up metal sheets around cement blocks; a foolproof way not to bleed emotions ever again. I didn't think that was living either; more like experiencing the days and nights feeling slightly numb.

I'd been hurt many times before, but... I still believed in love. I still wanted what I'd never experienced before; a love that was genuine and pure. A partnership filled with respect, consideration, and a best friend I could flirt with every day. And I'd love to get married to that guy someday, too. To marry the one person who added to my life, not made it worse.

I glanced at my computer screen. Ryan was being honest about where he was currently in life, what he wanted, and what he was able to offer. He was also gentle, and kind, and so fucking sexy with his sandy-blond hair and beard. His tall, toned body, naughty smile, and eyes that revealed so much even when he said little. It was life dangling that golden carrot in my face, then yanking it away the moment I got closer. "You like him?" Bam! Gone. "Fuck you! You can't have him. Someone hurt him badly before. He will pull away the moment you get too close. He will distance himself. He will become elusive. He **WILL** hurt you!"

I rolled my eyes, ignoring my silly thoughts. I was so dramatic sometimes, but that's just how I felt. Life really was cruel sometimes.

Perhaps we shouldn't chat anymore. Perhaps we should part ways now before starting anything. Perhaps I shouldn't experience anything out of fear of getting hurt. If I did that, what's the point of living? I couldn't hide away forever for fear of the unknown.

I sighed wearily.

> Do you want to stop chatting?

> The idea that I might hurt you isn't sitting well with me. That doesn't mean I don't still want to speak with you.

> I just want to be very sure that I will communicate all the details.

> The easiest way to get hurt is by misaligned expectations.

Another reason to like him; he was honest and

open about what he wanted, and he wanted to go about it hurting no one in the process.

"I'm going to do it," I said out loud to nobody but my cat. She meowed at me and stretched.

I was playing with fire, and dangerously close to getting burned. But the voice was telling me to try something I'd never done before, and to see it as an experience to remember.

I had nothing to lose, and if those feelings of mine appeared, I'd end it with him.

Simple.

> Ok, deal. Let's chat and tell me all the details so I know what to expect (or not to expect)

I hurried to the venue; a coffee shop near Strand Beach. I stopped near the entrance and felt deflated. It was empty. For a moment I'd thought he'd changed his mind, but when I turned the corner, there he sat. He glanced up and at first it didn't seem like he recognized me. I smiled. He stood. We hugged. I felt awkward and nervous at the same time. He ordered me a coffee and sat down. We stared at each other. My heart thundered in my chest. I was sure he could hear it, but I was just being silly.

"How was the drive here?" I asked, quietly cringing at my stupid question. Of all the things I could've asked, I asked that. It's almost as bad as talking about the weather.

He chuckled. "The drive was pretty. The meetings I had were okay. I'm glad we're finally meeting."

"Me, too," I said.

We shared information about our background, and the conversation flowed easily. He had a calm demeanor about him that put me at ease. I'd watch his lips when he spoke, where he placed his hands, and how he moved his legs. I sensed no deception, no cruelty, and no alternative agenda with him.

"What do you want?" he asked.

We'd already gone over this. I'd told him I wanted a relationship within a D/s dynamic. I basically wanted a kinky relationship with lots of sex and still enjoy *vanilla* stuff with my partner. I needed a partner in crime. Someone I could speak to daily. Someone I could share my life with. Someone who enjoyed the same activities I did. I wanted a favorite person. I wanted MY person.

"I want intimacy," he added.

I knew this, but my eyes still narrowed.

"I want the intimacy that sex brings," he continued. "I want the hugs, the cuddles, the skin on skin, kissing, orgasms. I want that."

I crossed my left leg over my right. I wanted intimacy, too; I craved it. I missed having sex with a man; playing with myself and by myself was getting lonely and boring. I missed the feel-good hormones flooding my body during sex, and I wanted to experience these things with him. I looked forward to kissing him, touching him, hugging him, cuddling him, and lots of fucking. Just thinking about the possibilities made my heart beat faster.

"You want no relationship? No boyfriend girlfriend stuff?" I asked, making sure.

He shook his head.

"Will you at least still chat with me?"

"Yeah, sure, we can continue speaking like we have been."

Our conversations had been sporadic. "What about every day?"

He arched an eyebrow. "That's like relationship stuff?"

"More like proof of life," I said, smiling. "Just a hello, you're still around. How is it going? That kind of thing."

I could tell by his facial expression he felt smothered by the idea of having to reach out to me on a daily basis. To me, reaching out daily was like aftercare - to ensure we were both still happy and on the same page about what we wanted.

I internally shook my head; it was an experience. It was something I'd never done before. I would keep my heart shielded tightly and enjoy the intimacy he brought with him, whatever it may be.

The depth of his hurt saddened me, causing him to distance himself from others. My empath-side wanted to reach out to him and make him feel better. To show him there were still women out there who had pure intentions and wouldn't hurt him like that. Unfortunately, if someone wasn't in a place to receive these gifts, it would go unnoticed.

I needed to remember to meet him where he was, and not where I wanted him to be.

I had nothing to lose, and lots of sexy fun times to gain. It was my small, soft heart I was afraid of crushing, though. The possibility of hurting myself was real; I may become attached to him. I may care for him. I may even begin to love him.

"Okay," I said with a shrug. "Let's do this."

Thoughts of his mouth on mine jump-started a fire within me. I glanced at his hands and imagined them on my body, touching me. Then I glanced at his pants, and moisture pooled between my legs.

He leaned forward. "I'm trying to see if you're wearing panties." He grinned mischievously.

I laughed. In our messages, I'd teased him about not wearing panties. Then I'd sit next to him, and he could walk his fingers up my leg.

I glanced at the cameras and scooted my chair closer to him, ensuring my legs remained under the table. He leaned forward, his large hands feeling up my calf muscles, my knees, and then my thighs. My heart thundered in my ears. I glanced behind me, but there was nobody there. His hands traveled further up my thighs, near my moist folds. His fingers brushed lightly against them and parted them. He moaned when he discovered how wet I was and sat back again.

He cleared his throat. "When are you free?" he asked with a sly smile on his face.

"Friday," I said.

"Then I'll see you on Friday."

I smiled nervously. "See you Friday."

We parted ways soon thereafter with a quick peck on the lips. I headed for my car and climbed inside, my mind reeling about what exactly had just happened. It had been so long since I'd had sex with a man; I hoped I remembered how to do it. I knew I was being silly. I was forty-five. I knew what to do and how to do it. But the butterflies... The butterflies were forming in my stomach so fast; I hoped I could handle everything.

Ryan messaged every day for the next three days, providing me with proof of life. I couldn't help but smile. We confirmed Friday's time; I'd see him after his last meeting ended. I spent the time cleaning and neatening my place for his arrival.

> Busy finishing up the meeting.

> Okay.

> I'll let you know when I leave.

> Okay.

To say I was nervous was an understatement; I was excited, nervous, and everything in between.

I wore no underwear under my black dress, and when my cellphone pinged, letting me know my visitor had arrived, my heart threatened to burst out of my chest.

Ryan and I had spoken online for over three months. We kind of knew each other. We had one coffee together, and now we were about to have sex. It's insane. In the 'olden days' they would've labeled me a 'whore', a 'slut'. These days more and more women did this kind of thing and often. Some even had one-night stands. I couldn't go that far, though. I preferred having sex with the same guy for as long as possible. That way I got to know his body, and I got to know him, too. I preferred that kind of recurring connection.

I opened the door after he knocked.

"Hi," I said.

He entered my apartment, placing his car keys and cellphone on the counter. He was tall, toned, and sexy as fuck. I didn't know what it was about him, but it sent my blood pumping hot all throughout my body. He smell delightful, too. That natural body odor that was laced with his sexual energy and it oozed out of his pores.

"How are you?" he asked, with mischief dancing in his eyes.

"Good. Would you like something to drink?"

"Tea, please."

I made him a cup of tea and felt his eyes on me the entire time. He enjoyed a sip, then set the cup down on the counter. He stepped closer to me, his dark gaze raking up and down my body.

I had soft curves in all the right places. I was built for comfort. I was very cuddly. And I wondered whether my body was good enough, pretty enough, and all that. But as he approached with intent, my thoughts disappeared, and I didn't care.

He reached for me. His lips finding mine. All it took was a kiss. A kiss to light the fire, a kiss to awaken the sexual being inside of me, a kiss to melt the apprehension away.

I rocked onto my toes and wrapped my arms around his neck, pressing my breasts against his hard chest as he felt the curve of my sides, my breasts, and my ass.

Juices pooled between my legs, and I couldn't wait for him to find that sweet spot of mine. But for now, I'd enjoy his tongue in my mouth, and his hands all over my body.

"You have too much clothing on," he said, ending the kiss. He reached for the hem of my dress and pulled it over my shoulders. I stood naked before him, wanting to cover myself, but I stood there for him to see.

Ryan pulled his top off. "Take off my pants," he said. His tone was full of desire.

I glanced up into his eyes as I reached for his belt, slowly undoing it. I unzipped him and slowly pulled his pants off. Then I curled my thumbs in his boxers and moved them down and off his legs. His hard cock springing free near my face, almost taking out my eye.

"Suck it," he said.

I got down on my knees and covered him with my mouth. He tasted yummy. With one hand on his ass, another cupping his balls, and my hot mouth over him. I sucked his cock, feeling every part of him with my tongue and lips. I'd glance up now and then just to see his expression. He stared down at me with a look I didn't yet know, imagining it was nothing but his burning need.

He reached for my arms and helped me onto the counter, spreading my legs. I wanted to die in a puddle of my juices; a man going down on me and tasting my wetness was a different kind of man. And Ryan loved doing that, and he enjoyed doing it to me. Men like him were dangerous, but in a good way. The moment he inserted a finger; it sent me into that pleasurable zone I'd missed so much.

He stopped and kissed me; I tasted my juices on his lips. He ended the kiss, helped me off the counter, and bent me over, pressing my face into the counter, and entered me from behind. Slowly, I felt his cock slide inside, inch by inch. Slowly, I enjoyed his pleasurable wrath inside of me and his hands on my body. I didn't want it to end. I didn't want him to stop. And I hoped he could go on for a long time.

He stretched my pussy as he entered and started pounding into me over and over. I missed this feeling of being used and pleasured. He was gentle, yet firm. His powerful hands skillful in their touch.

When he exited, I felt his loss. I stood straight, but before I could turn around, he started kissing my neck from the back as his hands found my breasts. I raised my arms, allowing him better access, and combed my fingers through his hair.

"Go to the couch," he said against my cheek.

I felt disoriented, my smile widening, my knees weakening, and walked towards the couch.

"On your back here," he said, pointing.

I loved it when a man took control of the scene; knew what he wanted and went about it in a gentle yet dominant way. His movements were primal as he acted on instinct.

Once I was on my back, he crawled on top of me, pushing his cock against my opening, and entered me again. With my legs bent and against his chest, he went deeper. He gripped my wrists and held them tightly above my head.

My eyes rolled into the back of my head as he pounded deeper and deeper. He felt wonderful sliding in and out of me. The sensations sending waves of pleasure up my spine.

He stopped and pressed his lips to my pussy and ate me out again. His talented mouth and fingers pleasured my wet pussy, driving me crazy with eagerness.

He changed positions and now stood near my face. I sat up, and he gripped my ponytail as he deep throated me. I gagged with each thrust. The amazing thing for me was the more I sucked his cock, the wetter I became. After a lot of gagging and tears streaking my face, he led me to the bed where we'd have more space.

"I want you on your back," he said, and moved towards me. He thrusted into me and my body sang. All my nerve endings came alive with his body against mine. Then, when his powerful hands grabbed my wrists and pinning them above my head, I fell apart. With him holding me down like that with his body hard against mine turned me into jelly beneath him.

After a while, he stopped and pulled me against his side for a cuddle and a breather. His heart raced beneath my ear. Mine was beating against my ribs. I was out of breath, my skin tingled, and my mind soared. But that wasn't the end. Soon after our break, he thrusted inside of me again.

We enjoyed over three hours of intimacy, cuddling, and kissing. Normally, a first sexual encounter was awkward, not this one. This experience was one to remember. I enjoyed every part of his body, whether it was inside of me or on top.

When it was over, he finished his tea, and we cuddled naked on the couch.

"That was wonderful, thank you," he said.

"Mmm, that was good," I said, leaning my head on his shoulder and draping my legs over his. "What are your boundaries?" I wanted to know exactly how this was going to proceed. It's something I hadn't done before and wanted to understand more about what to expect.

"What do you mean?"

"I want to understand what's allowed within the space between us."

"Oh, well, there aren't any boundaries, really."

Hmm, that wasn't what I wanted to hear. "Are you pursing other women?"

"No."

"With you not wanting a relationship, am I allowed to go on dates?"

"Oh," he said, sitting straight and almost letting me go. "I can't expect you to be monogamous, but when you sleep with someone else, then we end."

I understood we could no longer see one another if I were to become involved with someone else. Sexual health was important to me, too. I was also monogamous, and it would feel like I was cheating on him if I met with other men. I wasn't speaking with other men anyway, therefore it was a moot point, but at least now I knew.

"How about we take it one day at a time?" I said.

"Sure," he said, pulling me closer.

Ryan left shortly thereafter, and I didn't hear from him again that day.

The next day, I didn't expect a message either. I understood this was a purely physical exchange between two consenting adults. It would've been wonderful to have heard from him though, and to continue with some kind of '*aftercare*' following such an intense and beautiful event we'd shared.

I continued about my day and didn't put my hopes up. I was watching television when my phone pinged, making me smile.

> Thank you for a fantastic afternoon.
>
> I can't stop thinking about yesterday, and it was lovely.
>
> I'm glad it was memorable.
>
> It was…

I was happy he didn't forget about me.

The rest of our exchange was pleasant, respectful, and full of kindness. We agreed to meet the following weekend again, and although we didn't chat every single day, he at least reached out twice during the week.

The following weekend, I got everything ready and slipped on my white dress with nothing else underneath. I undid all the buttons in front and opened the dress slightly so he could see my cleavage.

I flinched when he knocked on my door. I opened it, welcoming him in.

"Oh wow," he said, reaching inside my dress and cupping my breast. "Very nice." His smile stretched his face in two. He pulled me in for a hug and kissed me chastely. "How are you?"

"I'm good," I said. "And you?"

"I'm great," he said. His eyes flitted from my face to my cleavage. "You have way too much clothing on."

I smiled, pulling my dress up and over my shoulders. Desire flashed in his eyes as he drank in my nakedness.

"Seems I'm overdressed myself." He chuckled, stripping down to his birthday suit.

When he was naked I pressed my body against his and kissed him. The kisses were soft, gentle, and full of need. The need for connection, the need for intimacy, the need for satisfaction.

"I want you on the couch," he said, removing his jewelry.

A nervousness settled in my bones of what was about to happen. I sat down. He stood between my legs, pushing them apart. He had one hand on the couch near my head to keep his balance and kissed me while his other hand went between my legs and finger fucked me. The sensation of his fingers going in and out and his mouth covering mine as I gasped with each thrust sent me deeper into the moment.

He helped me sit up and stood before me. I knew what he wanted and leaned forward, covering his cock with my mouth. I slowly licked the tip, tasting his pre-cum, then I went down, covering as much of his cock as I could without cutting off my air supply. Up and down, I went, filling my mouth with his hard member.

Ryan changed positions, pushing my legs further apart than before, leaning closer and kissed me. The tip of his cock pressed against my moist pussy and, while he kissed me, he slowly pushed inside. Again, I gasped as he stretched me, filling me. The feel of him slowly going in and out of me was something I wished I could bottle to use on lonely nights. It was something a dildo or vibrator simply couldn't replicate. He thrusted harder, pushing himself all the way to the end inside of me. His kisses felt needy, like he wanted more, which fueled my need for wanting more, too. I wanted to complain when he ended the kiss, but decided against it. He pulled out and kissed down my body. He settled between my legs and skillfully sucked and licked on my little button and pushed a finger inside.

This man was going to be the end of me.

After playing with me for a while, he laid on the couch. "Place your knees here," he said, showing me where he wanted me. "You know what to do," he added with a wicked wink.

I enjoyed sucking his cock, and excitement flooded my system as I got into position with my bum in the air and closer to his body. I lowered my face and started sucking the tip of his cock. My movements were slow and precise. I ensured there was enough spit as I went down on him. He pushed two fingers inside my pussy, and as I moved up and down, he went in and out. His other hand rested on my head, so that when I moved down, he pushed down on my head, ensuring his cock went further down my throat, and his fingers went deeper inside of me. He'd let me go, allowing me to come up for air and did it again, each time he pushed my head further down so that his cock filled more of my throat, blocking my airway. Little by little, he went further down my throat until he pushed my face right up against his body.

"You're so wet," he said lustfully.

Me servicing him with my mouth like that was new to me. No other man had ever gone that far down my throat before. His cock was the perfect size and length, and because of the angle I was in, his cock went down easily. I loved sucking cock and enjoyed deep throat, but this was a different kind of deep throat; it was the deepest ever, making me the wettest I'd ever been.

Tears streaked my face, spit ran down my chin, and my juices dripped down the inside of my legs. He helped me up and gently pushed me back onto the couch and thrusted his hard cock inside my very-wet pussy as I took in deep breaths of air, finally filling my lungs.

My mind had slipped to that quiet place where I no longer thought. I drifted deeper and deeper into that place where I no longer needed to make decisions; I could just be and enjoy the moment. My pussy was so wet and swollen and with him pumping inside of me only made me want him more.

"Let's go to the bed," he said, helping me stand. "We need more space for what I'm about to do," he said playfully.

I nodded, standing on shaky legs. He laid down on the bed and stared hungrily at me. I crawled towards him and kissed down his body, licking and sucking my way down to his cock. The smell of sex hung in the air, adding fuel to my already burning fire.

I positioned myself in such a way he could reach me, and his fingers could find their way inside me, and I went down on him. Again, he pushed my head onto his cock, ensuring it went all the way down my throat. Up and down, I went. My pussy clenching each time his cock blocked my throat, making me gag and wanting to throw up.

We changed positions with him on top of me and pounded into me. I was going further into my dark bubble, into my safe space. He leaned forward and kissed me tenderly as he continued thrusting.

I wanted to touch him, to pull him closer, but he said to keep my hands near my head, and being a *'good girl'*, I obeyed. I watched him slam into me; his cock sliding in and out, filling me with each stroke. Then I stared at his face, and into his eyes; eyes I could never tell what color they were. Eyes that held the weight of what he'd seen. Then I stared at his body grinding into mine; a delicate dance as our bodies melding into one.

Then I closed my eyes and enjoyed his delightful assault on my body.

"Use your toy," he said, bringing me back to the present and handing me the vibrator.

For a moment, I didn't know what was going on. I'd been so deep in my dark corner it took me a second longer to register what he'd said. He'd moved once more, and his knees were near my right shoulder. I glanced to my right and smiled, glancing up at him as he pushed his cock into my mouth, inching it deeper down my throat. I inserted the vibrator and started pumping. Then with his free hand he stretched my dark passage, because that's where he wanted to go next.

My mind seemed to collapse in on itself with so much happening at the same time, but the sensations were delicious. His finger in my ass, my vibrator on and in my pussy, and his cock fucking my mouth and going down my throat, blocking my airway. I was nearing my orgasm. I managed to ask for permission to cum with his cock in my mouth, but he told me to wait. He pushed his finger all the way in my ass, his cock all the way down my throat, and my vibrator hit that button of mine, and the orgasm smashed into me so violently I had no time to register what had happened. And I enjoyed one delicious wave of satisfaction after the other.

It was a new sensation that I'd experienced. So much had happened to my body in such a short amount of time, and I wanted more.

After the waves of ecstasy subsided, Ryan propped my bum on top of a pillow, added lube to his cock, and pushed his way into my forbidden hole. I relaxed and allowed entrance. The deeper he pushed inside, the more nerve endings he struck, making me shiver with anticipation. I inserted the vibrator again, feeling completely full. He leaned closer and kissed me tenderly, a welcome softness before his next move.

He pounded into my ass over and over as I pumped my vibrator inside my pussy. Double penetration like this was sensory overload at its best. It's one of the best feelings, sending me further and deeper into my dark space. My mind had quietened a long time ago, but this, this sent me over the warm, soft edge.

Ryan's co-ordination changed as his orgasm struck, filling my ass with his heated seed. Once done, he settled beside me, still inside of me.

We laid still as our heartbeats slowed down. I removed the vibrator and basked in the afterglow of our enjoyable encounter.

"Ready?" he asked.

I nodded.

He slowly left my body. The feeling of him exiting was filled with sadness because that meant he'd leave soon. I knew I needed to live in the moment and enjoyed the cuddle while it lasted.

Our sweaty bodies stuck together; I had no complaints; it was a great workout. I'd skipped going to the gym that morning and counted this as my session.

We laid there; the silence between us comforting. My body slowly coming back to life as I became more present with my surroundings following the 'feel good hormones' surging through my body.

After a while, he got up and cleaned himself and enjoyed a glass of water. I used the bathroom and joined him on the couch for a last cuddle.

"That was," I said, smacking my lips together for effect, "wonderful." The grin on my face said it all.

He smiled too. "Yep."

I settled in beside him with my hand on his leg. We spoke about the events that had happened during our week and past experiences with previous partners. As I laid there listening to him speak, I felt a shift within me, scaring me. I realized I wanted more and quickly squashed the thought.

"Sorry to cut the visit short, but I need to go," he said, pulling me back into the now.

"Oh okay," I said, sitting up. "What are you up to for the rest of the weekend?"

"As little as possible tomorrow and then working on Sunday. You?" he said, getting dressed.

"Meeting a friend for lunch, and maybe a swim in the sea," I said, reaching for my dress and pulling it on.

Once dressed, he leaned forward and kissed me, followed by a quick embrace. "Thank you for today. It was nice. I especially enjoyed the deep throat, and stretching your ass." He smiled, unlocking and opening the door.

"It was wonderful," I said, feeling strange. "Drive safely," I added, closing the door behind him.

The moment I closed the door, something had changed. It was different. I felt something. Things felt strange. I swallowed hard, but couldn't help it, and choked on a sob. I blinked back the tears, telling myself I wouldn't cry, but telling myself one thing and my body doing another was beyond my control. I closed my eyes and imagined pulling up the shields I'd momentarily dropped by mistake. I didn't want to develop feelings for him. Not so soon.

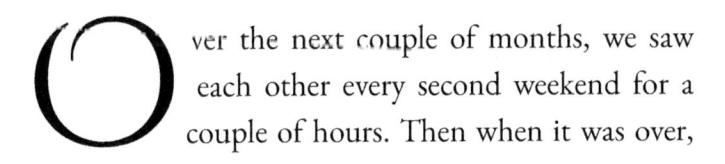

Over the next couple of months, we saw each other every second weekend for a couple of hours. Then when it was over, he'd leave, breaking that intimate connection with a chaste kiss and a sideways hug. And each time that happened, the sadness within me grew.

I didn't want to admit it; the feelings I had for him were growing, and each time I told myself that it was the last time. Then he'd message me wanting to come over, and I'd open my door, welcoming him inside, only to do it all over again.

"You don't look great," Glen said, staring at me with compassion in his eyes.

"Thanks," I said, rolling my eyes.

"I'm serious." He sipped his coffee. "What's going on?"

Glen was my best male friend. I always came to him for advice on men, and he came to me for advice on women.

"It's Ryan."

He arched both eyebrows. "You've developed feelings for him, haven't you?"

I averted my eyes. "Maybe."

"Pfft, that's not a *maybe*. That's more like a definite *yes*." He finished his food, pushing his plate to one side. "You're an emotional girly and an empath. You knew this was bound to happen."

"I know. It's been an incredible experience so far."

"And have you experienced enough?"

I nodded, blinking back tears. "What do I do? End things?"

He nodded. "You'll have to tell him. It's not fair to you or to him."

"But then I won't see him again."

"It's for the best. He can't be with you the way you want."

"I know," I said, sighing and rubbing my eyes. "I don't feel like going back onto those dating apps."

He chuckled. "You and me both."

"But you're dating that girl," I snapped my fingers, "what's her name?"

"It's over," he barked.

"What? When did this happen?"

"Last week."

"Why? She was nice."

"She had someone else's dick in her."

"You're joking. I can't believe it. She was the one who said the *'I love you's'* first."

"I know. That's why I'm so pissed."

"So, we'll both be single again."

"Looks that way," he said, sounding as deflated as I felt. "Get out before things get worse for you. You know you can't carry on with this if you've developed feelings for him. You were aware of the risks going into this. It's nobody's fault you've changed how you feel. It's better to get out now before both of you get hurt."

I stared at him. He was right. "It's been a wonderful experience, though." I grinned. Then my smile disappeared. "I'm seeing him tomorrow."

"Will you message him or tell him when you see him?"

"I want to do the chicken way out and message him."

Glen grumbled something unintelligible.

"You know I'll start crying before the words have even left my mouth. If I text him, I can think of the right words to say." I folded my arms and pouted.

"Do what's best for you and soon. The longer you drag this out the worse it will become." He finished his coffee. "I must run. Let me know how it ends." He paid his half of the bill, kissed my cheek, and headed for his car.

> Morning, were you able to beach walk today?

> Hey you! Yes. And it was good.

> About tomorrow…

> What's wrong?

> I've started to develop feelings for you and think perhaps it's best if we end things. I'm becoming too emotionally attached, and I don't want either of us to get hurt. I hope you can understand I now need to protect myself. I wanted to text you this first before tomorrow. I wouldn't want you to come here just for us to end things…

…

Those three dots flashed on my screen for a long time. It was at least five minutes when the dots disappeared, without leaving a response.

I swallowed hard and bit down on my lip. I'd rather feel physical pain than endure the pain in my chest.

"Shit!" I mumbled to myself, placing my cellphone on the counter beside me. He wasn't going to respond.

I continued with my day, checking my phone occasionally, but there was no response from him.

That evening, there still wasn't anything. The next morning, nothing.

Two, three, four, ten days had gone by and still no response.

No response *was* the response.

Him not replying told me everything I needed to know; whatever it was. As much as I wanted him to write something for closure, I had to accept his non-response as the closure.

I felt bad for ending things, but we both knew the consequences if I developed feelings for him; and I did. Ending it was the best thing for both of us. It had to be done.

"Have you heard from him yet?" Glen asked, pushing his feet deeper into the beach sand at Strand.

"No," I said, handing him his coffee and sitting beside him.

"How long has it been?"

"Over a month."

"Already?"

"Yep, time flies when you're single, remember."

"Ha!" he said, and fake laughed.

"How's the new girl?"

"Good, I have a date tonight." He wiggled his eyebrows.

"You're disgusting." I jokingly bumped into his shoulder.

"That's why we're friends." He grinned. "What about you? Back on dating apps?"

"No," I said, shaking my head. "Giving all that a break. Focusing on myself. It's all I can manage right now. I need to get over him."

"Good. Don't worry. The guy who's meant for you will come at the right time."

"Ugh, you're so philosophical. When did this happen?"

"Since I plugged myself into this professor."

We laughed. His new girl was a professor at the university near where he lived.

"As long as you're learning something from her."

We sat in silence, enjoying our coffee and the ocean in front of us. It was a stunning day, and as much as I tried to focus on the moment, I couldn't. I thought of Ryan; I hoped he was okay and wondered whether I'd ever hear from him again. I'd love to hug him one last hug, one last kiss, one last... but I knew that wouldn't be right. We were over and I had to accept it for what it was.

One month turned into two, then four, then six, then eight. A lot of time had gone by, and I'd slowly started forgetting about Ryan. I forgot his smell, his body, his naughty smile, how his hands felt on my body. I forgot it all.

I downloaded the dating apps, joined them for a day or two, then deleted my profile. Nothing had changed. And the same guys were still on from three years ago. Dating today provided too many options, and too many *'fish in the sea'*. On one hand, this was good news because one didn't have to stay with someone if it wasn't working. One could move on to the next person, but it also meant there was no more loyalty. Nobody worked at keeping the relationship. Things ended prematurely and before anything really got started.

To forget about men and dating apps, I treated myself to a shopping spree. I hadn't bought myself anything in a long time and I needed a treat. As I walked the aisles in one clothing store, my cellphone vibrated. I reached for it out of my bag and almost dropped it.

It was him…

> Hi. I know it's been a while.
>
> How are you?

I stared at the screen. My thoughts raced. My heart thundered against my ribs.

Why now? I thought to myself.

He didn't forget me.

> Hey there. It's been a really long time... I've been good. You?

> ...

Those three dots flashed on my screen, and I didn't want to look at them anymore. It was almost too painful to relive the last time that had happened.

But instead of the dots disappearing, his message appeared.

> I needed time to myself to reflect. I needed the time to heal a little more than I was. I needed the space to decide what I wanted out of life and how I wanted to go about doing things. I'm not completely the same as I once was, but at least I now have the capacity to heal alongside someone. Have I missed the chance? Have you moved on? I won't be upset if you have. I'll understand....

Tears flowed down my cheeks. His message struck a chord, bringing all those emotions I'd pushed deep down back up to the surface. I wiped the tears away so that I could see what I was typing.

> I'm genuinely happy for you and that you've moved forward in a positive and healthy way. Would you like to grab a coffee sometime?

> Friday at 5pm at the same coffee shop we met?

> Sure… see you then

The days came and went, and I couldn't wait for Friday to arrive. I found him in the same spot he sat in all those months ago when we first met. His face lit up when he saw me. He stood and closed the distance, pulling me into a warm embrace that lasted minutes.

"Would you like something to drink?" he asked.

"Please, I'll have a hot chocolate."

Once he sat down and gave me my drink, we spoke for hours. He explained why he had to disappear and why for so long. I understood. He had trauma from his past he needed to work through, as did I. We were human and needed to move through our scar tissue slowly and thoroughly.

"How are you doing?"

"Good," I said. Then gave a brief update on what I'd been doing.

I glanced at the clock, and we'd been there for four

hours already. When I looked at him again, he wore an expression I couldn't decipher.

"What's wrong?"

"I'd like to take things slowly with you. If you still have feelings for me and want to do this."

My heart stuttered in my chest. My smile reaching my eyes. "Yeah," I said, snuggling up against him. "I still want you."

"Good," he said. Then he chuckled. "Are you wearing any panties?" he asked, glancing at my shorts.

I grinned and uncrossed my legs under the table. His large hand landed on my thigh and moved to the inside. His fingers walked beneath my shorts and on my skin. His fingers brushed against my naked pussy lips. He groaned and glanced at me; his pupils had dilated, and a sly smile played on his lips. Unlike last time, where he did nothing, now he inserted two fingers inside. I gasped, scooting lower in my seat and opening my legs, giving him all the access he needed.

Voices outside caught our attention and a group of cyclists entered the coffee shop.

Ryan removed his fingers and adjusted his cock in his pants.

I fixed my shorts.

"Maybe we can continue this elsewhere." His smile reached his eyes. "Maybe we can have dinner together. Maybe I can spend the night?"

Hope blossomed in my chest. He'd never wanted to do *relationship* things with me, which told me he was serious about us moving forward together as a couple.

"I'd love nothing more," I said, grabbing my bag.

Speed Dating

BRIAN & JULIE

"Are you sure we want to do this?" I asked Maddy, my best friend.

"Of course," she said, rolling her eyes. "How else are we going to find boyfriends?"

"You already have a boyfriend." I arched an eyebrow.

"No," she drawled. "He didn't want to make it official."

"You're going to ruin things if you come with me."

"He should've thought of that before leaving me. I asked if we could make plans together but he didn't want to. Instead, I'm here with you. So, technically I'm single." She shrugged nonchalantly.

"Why don't you speak to him about it?" I asked, losing patience. Maddy had a wonderful guy she'd just started dating. I didn't understand why she wanted to come with me speed dating. As far as I was concerned, I was the only single girl between the two of us.

"I've already spoken to him about it and he shrugged it off. If he was serious about me, he would've answered me. He should've taken my feelings into consideration. But no, he shrugged. He ignored me. He made plans to go hunting with his buddies. And now I feel our relationship means nothing to him." Her anger rolled off her shoulders, and I could almost taste it.

"Men," I said, rolling my eyes. "I don't understand why they behave like that. You're cute, have a great job, an apartment. What's not to like? You've already told him you want to date him. So, why behave that way?"

"Exactly. I don't get it either. Anyway, I'm over it, and over him. Now come." She hooked her arm around mine. "Let's get dressed and see what the gods bring us tonight," she said, wiggling her eyebrows.

It only took us two hours to get ready and drive to Tiger's Milk in Somerset West, who were hosting this event; ***Love Sucks on Valentine's.***

Maddy wore a light blue, knee high sun dress that accentuated her full figure. I wore a dark gray skirt that reached my ankles, and a shoe-string top that had a built-in bra. We looked sophisticated, classy, with a hint of sexy.

She parked her car in the nearest spot we could find and headed towards the front door. There was a long queue outside since we were early and they hadn't opened the venue doors yet.

"Not much talent," Maddy whispered as we traversed down the sidewalk, passing the queue of men and women. "Oh wait, look Julie," she said, "he's kinda cute."

The guy she stealthily point at saw us and grinned. She quickly lowered her hand. But he'd already noticed us talking about him. He had a kind, yet naughty grin that matched his smiling blue-green-colored eyes.

After we passed him and were out of earshot, I laughed. "Yeah, he's cute. Now stop pointing and bringing attention our way."

"At least he knows we think he's cute, and he saw us. Maybe he'll come talk to one of us," she said with a shrug.

We stood at the back of the line and waited all but five minutes when it moved forward.

We reached the front door and greeted by a large woman sitting behind a desk. "Name?" She barked without looking up.

"Maddy Swanson."

"Here," the woman said, handing Maddy her badge. She glanced up at me. "Name?"

"Julie Nomad."

The woman nodded and mumbled to herself. "Here's yours," she said, smiling at me.

I took the badge from her and smiled back.

"This way," Maddy said, grabbing my hand and pulling me along. "Let's get a drink. They're free." She waved her badge near my face. "Get me my usual, will ya. I'm just going to the bathroom."

"Fine, but don't take forever. Your makeup is perfect." I watched Maddy skip into the ladies' bathroom and shook my head. She was crazy, but I loved her. I headed for the bar area to get us something to drink. "I'll have a mimosa, please," I said to the bartender. "And my friend will have a whiskey and water."

The cute guy from the queue stood beside me. "I'm Brian, by the way," he said, proffering a hand.

"Julie," I said, shaking his hand. Thank goodness it was dry. I hated shaking a man's cold, damp hand; ick.

"How many of these things have you attended?" he asked.

"This is my first one."

"Here you go," the bartender said, pushing two glasses my way. "What can I get you?" he asked Brian.

"A beer," he said to the bartender. "So, your first one, hey? This is my second."

"I take it the first one didn't go well if you're back?" I reached for my mimosa.

He chuckled, and it sounded good. Some men had that sexy laugh that make a woman want to curl up in his lap and kiss him. He had one like that; a chuckle that made my arms pebble and my legs tingle.

"It went well. We even went on a second date, but then she kept complaining about her *husband* and the things he wasn't doing for her. That's when I realized she was still married."

I choked, almost spitting my drink all over him. I reached for a paper napkin, wiping my mouth, and swallowed the rest of the drink.

"You okay?" he asked, grabbing more napkins on the far side of the bar counter. "I'll try not to be funny and make you laugh." He chuckled, handing me the napkins.

"I'm fine." I dabbed my mouth and chin. "I'm good," I said, trying not to choke on my spit. "Sorry that happened. I guess one doesn't really know they're married until we interact with them on a personal level."

"Yeah," he shrugged, "it's cool, though. Life must go on."

Brian had that rugged, yet handsome, look about him. Messy, dark blond hair with a beard. His eye color seemed to change; I didn't know if it was dark green or blue-green. Perhaps it changed with his mood. And he had an almost upperclass English and American accent mixed with South African. It was weird; I suspected he had traveled and often. He was also nice and tall.

"Yes, I agree with you. Life must always move forward," I said, sipping slowly on my mimosa. I didn't want to choke again.

"Here," the bartender said, handing Brian his beer.

"Let's get out of the way," Brian said, grabbing his beer, and moving towards a corner table as more people shuffled forwards to order their free drink.

I placed the two drinks on the table and glanced around the room. Maddy was nowhere to be seen.

"I think your friend has deserted you."

"Haha, I think so too." She'd probably bumped into some guy and was already getting his number.

"I'll keep you company until she returns," he said, grinning. "Unless you want me to go?"

"No," I said, smiling. "Stay and keep me company."

There was something in his expression; it was full of a dark desire that made my heart beat faster. It was the glint in his eye; that stare that stripped me naked. A smile that held promise of the unknown. It was a look filled with so much without saying a word.

We were at a speed dating event, therefore the chances of everyone's hormones being sky high was that much greater. I stared at his medium-sized lips;

they were the right fullness that I assumed kissed well. I licked my lips at the thought.

I stared at his eyes, his lips, and then his hands. He stared at my blue eyes, my lips, and my cleavage. I smiled. He grinned. I nervously sipped on my drink. He almost downed his. He reached for my hand, making me even more nervous than I was, and leaned closer.

"I want to kiss you," he said near the shell of my ear, and stood straight again to see my reaction.

My cheeks heated. I averted my eyes and shifted from one leg to the other. When I looked up at him again, his expression told me he wanted to do more than just kiss me.

I didn't know what to do. I wanted to kiss him, too. I wanted to taste those lips. I wanted to taste him. Kissing him in a place like this felt like the right thing to do. This was why I was here, to meet someone I liked and wanted to spend time with, and I liked Brian. And he liked me, too. I had nothing to lose.

I glanced over my shoulder. We were in a dark corner at the back of the room. There was another room behind us they used to keep all their cleaning equipment. I glanced back at him and tilted my head towards the room.

Brian reached for my hand. I allowed him to lead.

We entered the utility room. He closed the door and locked it. He removed his jacket and placed it on a shelf. I set my handbag next to his jacket. He closed the gap. He leaned forward and cupped my face. My mouth parted. His lips touched mine. I closed my eyes and gave in to him. My body melted against his. My hands roamed his body. His larger hands were all over my back and ass. Then his right hand found my breast. My hands went into his pants and I felt his naked ass, making me smile because that meant he wore no underwear; he moaned in the kiss.

I wasn't sure how far this would go. Would we end at just a kiss and touching, or would we go further? I had no condoms on me and hoped he did. I also didn't want to be perceived as someone who did this often; sleep with a guy on the first date. Not like I cared. I had needs and didn't feel guilty for going after what I wanted, but still. I didn't want him thinking I slept with all the guys I'd just met.

Brian pushed me up against the door, his leg pressed between mine. His knee moved near my pussy. I had to hike up my skirt so he could do so easily. His kiss was tender, yet filled with need. His hands were all over my body, and I wanted more. I wanted to feel his skin against mine. I wanted him on me and inside of me. Dirty fantasies filled my thoughts, and I wanted him to fulfill them.

Then Brian ended the kiss and stepped back, shaking his head as if dispelling thoughts. I licked my lips and combed my fingers through my messy hair, redoing the ponytail. His eyes raked up and down my body. He wiped his mouth dry and rubbed the hard-on in his pants. It looked like he wanted to let his cock free, but wasn't sure.

I glanced at the bulge in his pants, then at his face. "I've never done something like this before." My eyes flitted to the shelves behind him.

"Kiss someone in a utility room?" He chuckled.

"Yeah," I said, shrugging. "Do you still want to attend the speed dating?"

He shook his head. "No. I think I've found what I'm looking for."

My smile reached my eyes. "Me, too."

"You want to get out of here and go on a proper date?"

I nodded. "I'd like that."

We exited the cleaning room and found our table was still available and our drinks were untouched.

Maddy ran towards me. "There you are!" she yelled, bringing attention to us. "I've been looking everywhere for you." Her eyes flitted from me, then to Brian. She laughed. "You two look like you were stuck somewhere." She pointed at Brian's untucked shirt and the strap of my shirt that had fallen off my shoulder. "Are you staying?"

I glanced at Brian. "No, we're going on a date."

Brian nodded. "Lunch, maybe a walk on Strand Beach, then," he raised a shoulder, "sundowners?"

"Sounds perfect."

We did everything Brian suggested and ended up having sundowners at his place. I walked through his apartment, entering his second bedroom, which he'd converted into an office. He had framed photos on the walls showing him with his parents and his sister. I saw no photos of a girlfriend. His bedroom seriously needed a woman's touch; black bedding, small black carpet on white tiles, black curtains, black, black, black. At least his walls and floors were white, so I could see where I was going. His en suite bathroom had maroon carpets, maroon towels, maroon shower curtain. My eyes hurt after that.

"Are you done snooping?" he asked with a chuckle.

"Almost!" I yelled back, laughing. "I see no signs of a woman being here... ever." I giggled. "You need happier colors, something calm, maybe some crochet doilies on the toilet."

"There used to be one many, many, many years ago," he said, standing in the bathroom doorjamb.

I flinched, slamming the medicine cabinet closed.

"Find anything interesting?"

My cheeks heated. In the medicine cabinet he had anxiety medication, stacks of condoms, a razor, aftershave that smelled yummy, and shaving cream.

"Nope," I said, holding my hands behind my back like a naughty girly. "Just the usual. There's absolutely nothing special about your apartment." I grinned. "Nothing special at all."

"Well," he said, stepping closer, "I hope there's something special about me."

I shrugged nonchalantly.

He closed the gap and cupped my face. I closed my eyes and exhaled, pressing my left cheek into his hand. His fingers curled around my neck, sending all the hairs on my body to stand on end. When I opened my eyes, he was staring at me with a dark and dangerous expression. My mouth parted. I'd forgotten about the sundowner and wanted to drink him instead.

He leaned forward, bruising his lips lightly against mine. I wrapped my arms around his neck, pressing my body against his. He moaned in the kiss. Our tongues teased, our hands roamed. My core tightened. I wanted to get dirty with him, only to shower and get dirty all over again.

He ended the kiss, then kissed me chastely, and pulled away. When he opened his eyes, a fire burned in his expression. "There's so much I want to do to you." His smile matched his naughty eyes. "And all weekend. But I think tonight we'll only indulge in sundowners."

"Okay," I said, smiling, and feeling relieved. It was too soon jumping into bed with him, no matter how much chemistry we shared. Sometimes having chemistry of the flesh ran cold, leaving nothing behind; but chemistry of the mind always set the body on fire and that's the relationship I wanted; something that lasted long after looks faded. I hoped what we shared would become something meaningful.

I followed him to the living room, and we sat on a couch near the window looking out onto the estate dam. Music played in the background. His tiny dog, a French bulldog, sat in his basket in the corner, watching us with those cute-sad-puppy-dog eyes.

We spoke about our jobs, and where we saw ourselves in the future.

"You're on the road to owning your own business," I said, genuinely excited for him.

"Yes, there are still one or two things I need to finalize, and that restaurant is mine." Brian was a manager for a different restaurant and would resign from that position. He had all the experience necessary to run his new business, and his best friend would provide the capital and be his silent partner. "It will all go through within the next couple of months."

"Very cool," I said, happy for him.

"What about you?" he said, pointing at me. "You're on your way to owning your practice."

I beamed. "Yeah, my own physiotherapy practice." I was a joint partner with a colleague and about to break away to go on my own. I was waiting for the lawyers to send the contract through.

"Here's to our future." He raised his glass. We clinked and enjoyed a long sip.

The comfortable silence stretched between us.

"I've enjoyed my time with you, Julie."

"Me, too."

"I'd like to see you again."

"Do we have to end the evening?" I glanced at the clock.

He stared hungrily. "Before we continue with anything else, there are things I haven't shared with you yet."

I sat straight on my side of the couch. "Yeah? Like what?" I suddenly felt nervous.

He glanced out of the window. "I'm worried I'll scare you away... it's happened before."

"Scare me away?"

He nodded.

I laughed. "What can you say that will scare me away?" I raised a shoulder. "Well, it's going to come out sooner or later, won't it? So, just tell me now. Rip off the proverbial bandaid."

"I enjoy being in control, especially in the bedroom."

I nodded. "Okay, tell me more." I think I knew where he was heading with this.

"I like to own my partner. I enjoy doing things that aren't exactly 'vanilla'." He waited for me to react. I didn't. Instead, I stood and went to him. I stood between his legs, pushing against his knee so he'd open his legs wider.

"Control me. Own me. I like doing non-vanilla things."

His pupils dilated. He stood and grabbed my shoulders, gently pushing me backwards, giving him space.

"You sure you want to do this, now? We've only just met."

"I know. I like you, Brian. I want this, and I'd like to try now. If you do something I don't like, then we won't waste each other's time by dragging it out."

"Okay," he said, one side of his mouth curved upward. "Take your clothes off," he continued, removing his shirt.

I did as instructed and left my folded clothing on the single chair in the corner. I stood naked in the middle of his living room with my hands behind my back.

"You've done this before?" he asked, circling me, inspecting me.

"Yes," I said, smiling, with a twinkle in my eye. "Just a little."

He stopped in front of me and pinched both nipples. "Tell me if it gets too much."

"Okay."

"Yes, sir."

"Yes, sir," I said, closing my eyes as he pinched my nipples harder. My mouth parted when his wet lips covered my right nipple and his tongue circled it. I flinched slightly when his teeth bit down on my nipple, sending a current down to my core.

"You like that?"

"Yes, sir."

His right hand gripped my hip and his left hand went between my legs.

"Hmmm, so wet."

"Uh-huh, yes, sir."

"Good girl."

All it took were those two words for me to become wetter than I already was. Then, when his fingers danced across my wet folds, he grunted his pleasure.

Then he inserted his fingers, tearing a gasp from my lips.

"Hmm, yes, I want your sounds, I want your wetness, I want everything you want to give me."

"Yes, sir. That feels so good."

Brian started pumping his fingers into me, and his other hand rubbed against my clit. The sensations pulled me closer to the edge. Then he stopped. I groaned. He flipped me forward and spanked my ass.

"No complaining," he said, chuckling.

"Yes, sir," I said, giggling.

"Hands on the couch."

I did as he asked.

"Spread your legs."

Again, I obeyed. He parted my pussy lips and pressed his face into me. His tongue darted in and out as he sucked my clit. I squirmed with delight. He spanked each ass cheek, then continued sucking my pussy.

"You're so wet," he said into my core. "I love it, and you taste divine."

I gave in to the feel of his hands pushing my pussy-lips apart and his warm mouth on me. Then he gripped my hips and moved me onto the couch.

"Legs open," he said, removing his jeans. "Wait," he added and disappeared down the corridor. He returned a moment later with a box of condoms. He opened a box and removed a wrapped condom, tearing the packaging off, and covered his hard cock with it.

I stared at him and his large equipment. It was a beautiful cock, the right length, the girth wasn't too big, just perfect. I would love to taste him. I licked my lips.

"I'd love for you to suck me off, but for the rest of the time, I'd like things to be more vanilla. I want to go slow and sensual. I want you to know me better and to trust me," he said seriously. "I'd love for us to reach a point where I don't need these," he threw the box of condoms on the table. "I love feeling skin on skin. But tonight is about us doing something kinky so that you're comfortable with the things I enjoy, and also for us to get to know a little more about each other's body."

"Yes, sir, I'd like that very much." I reached for him.

He positioned himself between my legs, slapping his sheathed cock against my pussy. "Are you ready for me?"

I love that he asked for consent again, even though I'd already given it. That told me so much about his character and that I could trust him.

"Yes, sir," I said, leaning back and relaxing.

He pushed the tip of his cock inside, stretching me. He inched in slowly, then pulled out, but right before he exited completely, he entered again. In and out, in and out. He continued slowly so that I could get used to the feel of his cock. It felt wonderful; his warm body against mine, his cock inside of me, him moving in and out. All these sensations left me feeling alive. My body was hyper-sensitive. The waves of pleasure pushing and pulling me closer to the edge.

I reached between us and rubbed my clit as he pounded into me. He leaned closer and kissed me. Neither of us lasted long after that. His thrusts became harder and deeper, and I rubbed my clit harder and faster. The orgasm smacked into me, and as I clenched my pussy around his cock, he came. His movements slowed. He shuddered and collapsed on top of me. There were a couple of aftershocks of my orgasm, and I squeezed around him again, making him moan with delight.

"That was yummy," he said, moving us around on the couch so that his body enveloped mine.

"It was." I adjusted my body so that I could kiss him without hurting my neck. "Thank you, sir." My smile reached my tired eyes. I yawned.

He kissed my temple. "You might as well stay the evening."

"I agree, then I can get all the cuddles I need." I smiled lazily, glancing at the clock. "It's already one in the morning."

"No ways," he exclaimed, leaning on his elbow to see the time. "So it is. Well, that's settled then. You're staying. We both get cuddles and a good night's rest." He sat up. "Let's go to the bed though. This couch is not comfortable to sleep on."

I sat up and took the hand he held out for me, and followed him to his bed. I grinned to myself; he had a nice bum.

"I'll pick you up at seven," Brian said, kissing me chastely.

"I can't wait," I said, opening my apartment door.

He stood there like he didn't want to leave. Perhaps he worried I'd disappear. "Okay, I'm going." He backed away, glancing over his shoulder. "I'll see you later."

"Wait," I said, reaching for him and pulling him closer. My lips bruised his, while my tongue conveyed I wanted something more. "There, now that's a better kiss."

He chuckled; I liked the sound of that, making me smile.

"I'll see you later," I said, pinching his sexy bum.

"Bye." He winked.

"Bye," I said, waving.

I entered my apartment and stopped dead; Maddy was on the couch, naked.

"Maddy, where are your clothes." I closed the door. "Brian could've seen your naked ass."

She stirred, sitting up, and yawned. "He can look. You know I don't mind being naked." She grinned. "I also got lucky," she said, wiggling eyebrows. "Devon left about an hour ago, giving me the best workout I've had in my life."

"Ugh, you're so gross. I can't believe you did it on my couch." My face contorted in disgust; I loved my bestie, but sometimes her behavior was appalling. "I need to sit there later." I leaned forward to see if there were any wet spots, luckily there weren't. "Why are you here, anyway? What's wrong with your apartment?"

"Ugh, I left my apartment keys here. I know, I know," she said, pulling on clothing. "If my head wasn't on, I'd lose that too." She searched for something. "Yes," she found her panties, pulling them out from between the cushions and waved them in the air. "I take it you had a good evening?"

"I did, we did." I gushed, remembering the moments we spent together.

"What? Is that love stamped all over your face?" She scrunched her face in disgust.

"What? No, lust maybe. But we might be on the road to something more."

"Aaah, I'm happy for you, my friend." She pulled me in for a hug.

I cringed. She was still naked and sticky. "You smell like sex. Have a shower and then hug me." We laughed.

"Wench. Coffee first. You know I can't do anything without my morning dose." She pushed me to one side, almost falling over when she pulled on her underwear, and made us coffee.

Seven o'clock came and went. By eight, I kicked off my shoes. He wasn't coming. I couldn't understand why, though. I thought we had a great time and he wanted to see me. He seemed interested in me. He'd said he was going to take me to dinner; I didn't think he'd lie or he wouldn't have planned anything for today. He would've told me if he'd changed his mind.

I hated these thoughts swimming in my head. Doubt plaguing my mind. Unfortunately, I'd been here before, and I was just protecting myself. I was sure Brian wanted to see me again.

I picked up my cellphone and realized I didn't take his number and he didn't have mine. I sighed; I couldn't believe it. We'd been so smitten with each other that we hadn't bothered to exchange digits.

We're such idiots, I thought to myself.

Maddy would roast me for this. She'd stayed for most of the day and left before I got ready. Apparently, her head was on correctly and got her dates number within the first half an hour of meeting him. They'd be seeing each other tonight again, too.

I flinched when a knock sounded at my door. Jumping up, I opened the door and smiled. "You made it!"

"I'm sorry," Brian said, entering. Sweat dripped down the sides of his face and his shirt was damp. "Stupid flat tire," he said, raising his dirty hands. "It took me forever to change it, and when I wanted to tell you I'd be late, I wanted to kick myself for not taking your number."

"I know," I said, waving my cellphone. "I noticed that."

He kissed me, leaving his dampness on my face, but I didn't make a show about wiping it off. I was relieved he was okay, and he'd arrived.

"You want something cold to drink?"

"No," he washed his hands quickly, "let's go. They moved our reservation to eight-thirty." He dried his hands and reached for me. "You ready?" He glanced at my naked feet.

"Hold that thought." I pulled on my shoes, grabbed my handbag, and slipped my hand in his. "Now I'm ready."

Dinner was delicious. We ate at a fancy Italian restaurant where men had to wear blazers. Brian was sexy in his suit, and I wore a black cocktail dress that hugged my fuller figure.

Brian paid even though I said I'd pay my share.

"You can pay for the next one?"

"MacDonalds it is," I said, laughing. "Just kidding. I don't mind." We both earned a similar income. Therefore, I didn't mind that we shared costs.

"What would you like to do next?"

"Well, I was thinking about all that stuff from last night, and I want more. If that's what you want?"

His eyes held mischief. "Let's go."

The drive back to his place, I couldn't keep my hands off of him. My fingers walked up his thighs and between his legs. He shook his head, stealing glances my way.

"Someone needs a few whacks to the bum." He grabbed my hand when I brushed my fingertips lightly against his already hard cock and squeezed. "Keep still."

"Yes, sir," I said, leaning closer, and rested my head on his shoulder.

He smirked, still holding my hand.

It felt like we were moving too fast, but it was comfortable. It's like I'd known him for years. I could be my goofy self around him and all he'd do was laugh at me or join in on the joke. He didn't make me feel bad about myself or embarrass me.

We arrived at his apartment, we unbuckled, but instead of him letting my hand go, he made me crawl over the seats and out his side. He continued to hold my hand as we traversed up the path and to his apartment on the third floor.

A nervousness bubbled in my chest when we entered, and everything was dark. He closed the door behind me, still holding my hand, and I squeezed tighter. I didn't want him letting go.

He turned around, let go of my hand, and pressed my shoulders against the wall. His hands moved from my shoulders, down my breasts, the curve of my waist, and hips. He gripped my hips and spun me around, making me gasp.

"Press your hands and face against the wall," he said.

I did as instructed. My breathing came in short, shallow breaths. I pressed my face against the wall and stuck my bum out. He lifted the hem of my dress, pulled my panties down, and smacked each ass cheek five times with his bare hand. It stung where he smacked me, but I dared not make a sound. When he was done, he rubbed the areas in a gentle circular motion.

"Feet apart." His hand moved to my front, and a finger entered me. His breath moved my hair, tickling my neck. He stepped closer and kissed my neck and down my shoulder. He caught the strap between his teeth and pulled the strap off. "I want this off." He let go of me and stepped back.

A light came on, illuminating the living room.

"I want to watch you undress," he said. His stare went from my eyes to my breasts, then down my body as I stepped out of the dress. I removed my underwear, placing the items neatly on a chair. "Beautiful."

We stared at each other for what felt like ten minutes, but I knew it was only seconds. He moved with purpose, closing the distance. His eyes were dark with desire, his hands itching to touch, his body hard; his cock harder.

He gripped a fistful of my hair and pressed his body against mine, slamming us against the wall behind me. I felt him move against my front as his mouth covered mine. I melted into him. He was possessive and all-consuming and I allowed myself to be consumed by him; he was addictive.

Then he ended the kiss and stepped back. "Arms up," he demanded.

A nervousness settled in my bones, along with

excitement. I leaned against the wall and raised my arms above my head.

He undid his belt and pulled it out of his pants. He stepped closer and tied my wrists with his belt. It was surprisingly soft against my skin even though the edges cut. I moved slightly, realizing my hands were stuck there. I glanced up, noticing for the first time the hook in the wall, strategically placed, and his belt fit perfectly.

Under normal circumstances, I'd be panicking that I couldn't get free, but I trusted Brian. We'd only known each other for two days, but my nervous system felt calm around him. I didn't get a sense he wasn't trustworthy, was emotionally unavailable, other women didn't pull his attention away, nor did I get psycho vibes from him.

Brian stepped closer, holding something in his hands. Then I heard it buzzing, followed by his hands near my soaking pussy.

"I want you to cum hard for me," he said. His tone sending goosebumps all over my body. Then he pressed the vibrating magic wand against my clit. It must've been on the highest setting because the moment it touched me, it sent shock waves through my body, threatening to unravel me. I came quickly, and I came hard. It was a good thing he'd tied me to the wall, otherwise I would've collapsed into a puddle of my juices on the floor.

After I came not once, but three times, Brian released me from the wall, bent me over the couch and spanked me five times on each ass cheek. Each spank was harder than the first, sending my thoughts into darkness where there was nothing but softness and tenderness. His gentle hands caressed the tender areas as he lightly tickled my back.

He helped me stand and turned me around. He was naked and his cock was hard, ready for me. I licked my lips. He grinned. I sat on the edge of the couch, covering him with my warm mouth. He grabbed my head and each time his cock went down my throat he pushed my head down harder, ensuring his cock went all the way down my throat, blocking my airway. And each time he did that, I felt the couch get wetter beneath me. My body responded to his touch as if made for him.

Brian gently pushed me so that I fell back onto the couch and crawled on top of me. He pushed his cock against my soaking pussy, asking permission to enter. I nodded my '*yes*'. We weren't using condoms because I wanted us to be long term. I wanted us to be a couple. I wanted us to do everything together. By saying *yes* to enjoying skin-on-skin was risky because he could still turn around and dump me, but there was something in his eyes that told me he was in this for the long term, too. That he wanted me. That he wanted to explore this with me.

And he pushed inside. I felt him; every inch. I closed my eyes so that the only sense I focused on was touch and smell; and him. I focused on his body against mine. I focused on his cock thrusting inside of me. His breath against my skin, his beard against my chin, his lips on my lips; our tongues tasting each other. I focused on him, savoring the moment.

I wrapped my legs around his body and thrusted into him when he did so that he went deeper. My arms clung to his upper body. He leaned on his elbows, then grabbed my wrists, holding them above my head. His grip tightened on my hands as he pounded into me. I enjoyed the sensations, like lightning bolts surging through my body.

His movements became uncoordinated as he fought not to release too soon, but he couldn't help it. He pulled out and came all over my stomach and breasts; his heat against my skin made me smile. He shivered and moaned as he finished, then snuggled beside me.

"That was wonderful," he said, kissing my temple.

"Mmm," I said, licking dry lips. I turned to face him, careful not to let his cum drip all over his couch.

"Considering you licked me, does this mean I'm yours?"

He chuckled. "Oh absolutely," he kissed my forehead, "I think I'll keep you around for a while." He kissed me chastely.

My smile left my face as I stared at him. His smile disappeared, too. "I like you, Brian, I really do. I'm serious when I say, can we give this a go? A relationship. You know, really try to make things work?"

He nodded. "I'm also tired of mixed signals, tired of minimal effort, tired of confusion, tired of playing games, tired of inconsistency and inconsideration. I want a relationship that doesn't hurt before it's even begun."

Tears stung my eyes. "I want a best friend, a spiritual partner, and someone I can flirt with all the time. I want you to calm my soul and make me crazy in the flesh."

He grinned, kissing the tip of my nose.

"I want a favorite person," I continued. "My favorite pair of eyes, my favorite way to spend my lazy afternoons, my favorite name appearing on my phone."

"Deal. Let's give this a go, because I'm so tired of being single. Tired of going on dates. I want someone to enjoy life with. A partner in crime. I want it all."

"Deal, let's do that for each other."

6 Months Later

"I can't believe you're getting married," Maddy said, fixing her dress straps. "Can't believe you got me in this purple dress." She stared at herself in the mirror. "I look awful." She scrunched her face.

"It's lavender," I said, flicking her shoulder. "And I can't believe I'm getting married. Eeeek," I screamed.

"You make each other happy," she said, handing me my garter belt. "And you will choose each other every day. It's so cute, it's almost pathetic." She grinned. "Just kidding. I'm just jealous."

I secured my day collar around my neck. Brian had given it to me three months ago when he proposed. He'd said he wanted to spend the rest of his life with me and the sterling silver day collar was my engagement "ring". I didn't even bat an eyelash and jumped into his lap as I said *yes*. I wanted to spend every waking hour with him.

"He makes me happy," I said dreamily and twirled

my fingers around the day collar, "and I'll do everything I can to make sure he stays happy."

"That's what it's all about," Maddy said, nodding to herself. "I'm genuinely happy for you."

"How's your love life?"

"Ugh, let's not go there," she said, rolling her eyes into the back of her head. "I have a date tomorrow—"

"On a Sunday?"

"I know. We're going to a wine farm in Stellenbosch. Apparently, his father is some big-shot wine maker and they're revealing their latest wine tomorrow."

"Sounds fancy. You should've invited him to the wedding."

"No," she said, giving me the stink-eye. "You're family. He's just some guy I met on an app. He sounded so pretentious. I'll see how long I stay there." She shrugged. "I may or may not phone you to get me out of the date."

"Honey, I'll be on my honeymoon tomorrow."

"Oh yes," she said, looking worried.

"But still phone me. You know I'll be there for you."

"Thank you," she said with relief, but the look in her eyes held sadness.

"What's wrong?"

"You're growing up."

I burst out laughing. "We're in our forties."

"I know, but still, you're getting married and here I am, single."

"You'll meet your guy. Don't worry."

"Hope so."

"Girls! Are you ready?" The priest called, sticking his head in. "Brian is getting worried."

"I'm ready!" I said, heading for the open door, and ready to become Mrs. Brian.

About Last Night

JASON & MADDY

"Maddy?" Jason said, pulling me in for a hug.

"Jason?" I said, doing a double take. "You look different to your pictures." My frown deepened.

"Yeah, they're old."

And you're so much hotter than your pictures; I wanted to say but kept my mouth shut. I may have already embarrassed myself by staring into his bright green eyes. He was handsome in a different way. I knew that made little sense, but it made sense to me. His nose was a little skew and reminded me of a Roman soldier's, his top lip was smaller while his bottom lip slightly bigger, his jaw a little round but the beard covering it made him look older and wiser, and it gave him this look I was suddenly attracted to.

I continued staring at him.

"Anyway," he said, smiling, and glancing away. "You ready to come inside?"

I blinked and looked around. We were still in the parking lot. "Um, yeah, sure. Let me lock quickly." I locked my car, fixed my skirt, and nodded. "Okay, now I'm ready."

"Like I said on the phone," Jason continued, "my father is revealing a new wine tonight and I didn't feel like sitting through this thing by myself. I'm glad you came to keep my company." His smile didn't reach his eyes as he nervously glanced at the doors we were fast approaching. He opened one side of the double doors and held it open for me to enter first.

"Thanks," I said. My mother taught me to always thank the man when he treated me like a lady. That kind of chivalry had gone out of fashion; but not here.

"This way," Jason said, reaching for my hand.

We walked hand-in-hand along stone-brick hallways and entered a room filled with people sitting at round tables. There were easily a hundred people filling the room, and at the back was a long table where six people sat and they stared at Jason and me.

I felt uncomfortable beneath their watchful gaze and moved to Jason's other side, shielding me. He squeezed my hand as if realizing my discomfort.

The room was a cacophony of conversation, forks

hitting plates, and glasses clinking. It was only the table in the back that was deafeningly quiet.

"Jason?" A tall man said, standing, and approaching. "You never mentioned bringing a date with tonight," he jerked his chin in my direction.

"Yeah, um, this is Maddy. I've asked her to join me." He glanced nervously at his family, who stared daggers at me.

I moved behind him so that I was no longer in their firing line.

Jason's father grunted his disappointment and exhaled loudly. "Maddy, is it?" he said, grabbing my attention.

"Yes, sir," I said, moving out of Jason's shadow.

"I'm Hugo," he said, proffering a hand.

I shook his warm hand. He didn't let go. He stared at me with intense hazel-colored eyes. I let go first. Hugo smiled, his eyes lingered. My chest heated as flashes of a naked Hugo moving on top of me. I squeezed my eyes shut, expelling the thought, and when I opened them again Hugo continued staring at me as if he had witnessed my visions.

What was wrong with me? I was here with Jason.

I glanced at Jason, who made me just as flustered. *Dammit.*

Hugo and Jason's mother must've had him when they were young, because they were in their early fifties. Jason was only thirty-five. I didn't know why he wanted me. I was ten years older than him.

"We'll make space for you," Hugo said, calling servers over to add a plate beside Jason's. "Come," he added as his large hand found the small of my back, branding my skin there, and gently pushing me towards a seat.

When I realized the seat was beside Hugo, I swapped with Jason, who didn't seem to mind. If I sat between Hugo and Jason, my cheeks wouldn't stop glowing.

Jason leaned closer to me. "Sorry about earlier. Hugo can be a jerk sometimes."

"Don't worry about it," I said, squeezing his forearm. "I understand. They weren't expecting me. Why didn't you tell them I was joining you?"

Hugo stood up, pulling our attention, and made a speech about the latest wine they produced, along with the detail on how they went about doing it.

"My mom has been trying to set me up with her friend's daughter, Amanda," Jason continued, nodding toward a tall, busty blonde woman. She had a beautiful body, but her breasts spilled out of her dress, her face seemed a little off with her big lips, too thin nose, and large forehead. "We have nothing in common and whenever I speak to her, I develop a headache."

I burst out laughing. When I realized I was loud and the audience glanced my way, I covered my mouth with my hands. I felt heat on my left-hand side and noticed Hugo staring at me. I thought he was going to complain. Instead, he winked. That shut me up.

Jason patted my leg and leaned back in his chair, folding his arms across his chest. He kept giving me sideways glances, and a smile tugged at the corners of his mouth.

I scooted closer to Jason's chair so that Hugo could no longer see me.

A woman cleared her throat; Jason's mom. She narrowed her eyes at Jason, who shrugged.

Hugo finished his speech, the audience clapped, and he sat down. The servers placed the starters in front of everyone and Hugo said to *enjoy*.

"Is her voice that icky?" I said, in between delicious mouthfuls.

"Oh yeah," Jason said, glancing up at this poor girl. She cackled. I glanced up, my jaw dropping open slightly. "See, even her laugh makes my head hurt."

"Just imagine her in bed," I said, giggling. "Shame she can't help it."

"I know, but still. Her body might be an *eight*, but everything else is a *two*." He raised a shoulder. "Mom must just get over herself."

"Do they know you're on dating apps?"

He shot me a look that said it all: *No.*

"You're thirty-five. You can do what you want... can't you?"

He shook his head and turned his chair towards me. "I'm the eldest son. They have left this place to me," he glanced around the room, "and it's expected I do what they want. I've done everything they've wanted of me. But this, I won't accept the woman they've chosen." He shook his head in defeat. "I can't live my life in misery at work and at home. If work is going to suck, then I at least want to come home to a woman who will support me. Not ask me for my bank card so she can go shopping."

I squeezed his thigh. "I make my own money, so you don't have to worry about me," I said jokingly.

He turned and gave me a look that made me nervous. "I know. That's what I like about you. You aren't a trust fund baby. You make good money. Have your own place. You have a natural beauty that makes me weak. You're real, and you're someone I might want in my life."

Flattery got him everywhere. Unfortunately for him, I didn't take compliments well and just stared back at him with a smile I assumed made me look silly.

"Sorry, I know that's forward considering we met an hour ago, but you know what I mean."

"I do," I said, understanding what he meant; materialistic things meant nothing to me if the person giving them did so half-heartedly. The things I wanted from a man were more expensive; his time, his attention, kind gestures, consistency, supports me, communicates clearly, and wants to grow with me. Few wanted to put in the effort to do these things anymore.

When the main course was served, I excused myself to go to the bathroom. I'd had two whiskey and waters already and desperately needed to pee. I exited the main hall and walked down a narrow corridor, coming to a dead end.

Shit.

I crossed my legs when it felt like I was about to wet my panty and hurried back the same way I came. I turned the corner and walked into a wall of muscle.

"Are you lost?" Hugo asked, gripping my wrists against his chest after I used them to shield myself upon impact.

"I'm looking for the bathroom," I said, stepping back and trying to get my wrists free, but Hugo held tightly.

"They're that way," he said, glancing to the side. "Let me take you," he added, letting go of one wrist.

"You don't have to hold my hand," I said, glancing over my shoulder if Jason was looking, but he was speaking with his mom.

"I wouldn't want you getting lost again," Hugo said, chuckling.

I followed behind Hugo with my hand still in his, feeling like a child. We went left, right, and down a long corridor until eventually he stopped outside a door with the picture of a woman.

"I'll wait for you."

"It's unnecessary," I said, glancing the way we came. "I'm sure I can find my way back."

He arched an eyebrow. "I'll wait, princess. I don't want Jason worrying you've ditched him."

I sighed, made a show of rolling my eyes into the back of my head, and pushed the door open with my shoulder and hip.

Hugo chuckled, leaned against the wall, and stared down the corridor. He looked like a guard waiting for his prisoner.

I used the bathroom and washed my hands. The door opened. I looked up. Hugo entered. An uneasiness spread within me. I felt like prey beneath his gaze.

"Tell me if I'm mistaken," he said, raising his hands in mock surrender. "Do you want me to come in here and kiss you?"

I dried my hands with a paper towel, and swallowed hard.

Did I?

Did I want this fifty-something-year-old man in the women's bathroom with me?

I bit my lip. I did. If I was being honest with myself. I wanted this man. But I wanted Jason, too. It confused me.

My eyes flitted to the door, then back to him.

"I won't do anything you don't want me to do." He kept his arms in the air. "We can just kiss and then you can go back to Jason." He stepped closer until his shoes touched mine.

"What about Jason?" I asked.

Hugo grinned knowingly; as if there was something more to the story I knew nothing about. His dark gaze raking up my body. His tall body waiting for my touch.

Exhaling a frustrated breath; my thoughts went to my best friend's wedding yesterday. She had found her *'forever'*. I was happy for her. I wanted to find mine, too. Unfortunately, I didn't think behaving like this would get me anywhere, and right now, I had no limitations. No one had specifically instructed me not to do anything with anyone; I was single and could kiss whomever I wanted. This may become complicated if I were to continue seeing Jason, but I didn't know what was going to happen tomorrow. There was nothing wrong with living in the moment, and in the now.

I rocked onto my toes, pressing my breasts

against him, and snaked my arms around his neck. My fingers combed through his sandy-blond hair. His hands went straight to my ass, and he squeezed. He spanked one ass and pulled me closer into him so that I could feel the hardness between his legs. He leaned forward, pressing his lips against mine.

The kiss. It was full of need, full of want, full of desire. His burning hands roamed my body as he pulled against him. It felt like I was about to melt into him. He pushed me against the wall and pressed his knee between my legs.

"Ah," he moaned. "I want to taste the rest of you," he said, while kissing me.

He was a great kisser. Oh my gods, and his knee pushed right up into my moist center. I wanted to free his cock then and there.

Jason came into my mind's eye. *Dammit. What about Jason?*

"Stop thinking," he said, ending the kiss to look at me. "Nobody has to know anything. This is a onetime thing. And we're just kissing." He glanced down at my cleavage and licked his lips.

Hugo was a dirty old man, and as cringy as it sounded, I was attracted to him. His primal way of doing things was hot. His primal lust made me wet.

I reached for his pants and unzipped him, pushing

my hand inside. I gripped his hard cock in my hand and stroked up and down.

"Christ," he moaned, pressing his body against mine and ground into me. He had already removed his knee from my core and replaced it with his hand. He first rubbed me through my clothing, then found his way under my dress and into my panties.

"Christ, you're so wet," he said, kissing my neck. "I want to fuck you."

I undid his belt and button and his cock sprang free. I reached inside my bag and pulled out a condom.

"Wait! What are you doing?" he said, realizing I was about to slip it on him. "Really?"

"I'm sorry... I thought... Things were going one way... We don't have to." I lowered my hand. "Not sure what I was thinking." Feelings of embarrassment flooded my system, and disappointment in myself.

"Don't be sorry," he said, reaching for me. "I want to, believe me, I do." His naughty grin returned.

"Are you sure?"

He nodded.

I thought of Jason and doubt crept in. "I just met your son, just met you. I don't even know if Jason and I vibe, you know. But you, Hugo, we definitely vibe. What about your wife?"

I handed him the wrapped condom. He took it out of my hands.

"Don't worry about my wife. We're divorced. I'm single too."

"As long as we aren't hurting anyone."

"Jason won't be hurt or jealous when he finds out."

My eyes narrowed, not understanding what he meant. I wasn't going to tell Jason anything.

"*If* he finds out I'll say you seduced me," I said with a wicked wink. "Jason is sweet, but," I raised a shoulder, "I don't know if he has what it takes to handle me." I teased.

Now that there was distance between me and Hugo I could think straight and realized a few things. I lusted after Hugo; we had instant chemistry. Jason was sweet. He was a nice guy, but we had no instant attraction. Being with someone like Jason, that chemistry needed to grow between us. Right now, I didn't know if it was something either of us wanted.

He chuckled. "Yeah, blame me. I did seduce you." We stared at each other; the heat dancing before us, the fire raging higher. "Fuck it. I can definitely handle you." He tore the wrapper and removed the condom, placing it over his hard cock. "Lift your leg," he said, closing the distance between us.

I removed my underwear, placed my foot on the basin, and leaned against the wall. Hugo pushed the tip of his cock against my opening, grabbed my hips, and entered my heated core.

I gasped, feeling the stretch. Hugo pulled me onto him, making him go deeper. He grunted with each thrust. I gripped his shoulders for support and allowed him to pound into me.

When he started shaking and losing coordination, I ground my pussy into him and rubbed my clit so that I, too, could cum. He felt delicious inside of me as I milked his cock during my orgasm. He groaned, leaning into me and against the wall. His breath blowing my hair off my shoulder.

My raised leg started shaking, forcing me to lower it. Hugo pulled out and removed the condom, throwing it in the trashcan near the basin. I grabbed the cloth sticking out of his pocket and used it to clean myself, then tucked it back inside his pocket while he cleaned himself at the basin.

"You're such a dirty vixen," he said, staring at the now soiled cloth in his pocket. "I love it." He dried himself with a paper towel. "I want to see you again."

I washed myself and my hands. I fixed my makeup and spritzed some perfume. My panties laid on the floor and I bent down to scoop it up when Hugo grabbed my hips, pulling me into him.

"You're driving me crazy, woman. Did you hear what I said?"

"I heard you," I said, spinning around in his embrace, placing my wet panties in his pants pocket. "Think of me." I grinned. "I'd like to see you, too."

I sat down, needing to fix my dress, but it clung to my body and twisted around my waist. A cool breeze brushed against my naked pussy, making me feel exposed, and I quickly covered my knees with my dress.

Jason glanced at me and smiled. "You okay?" He eyed my legs.

"Hmm," I said, smiling.

Hugo sat down, winking at me before turning to speak with his ex wife, who continued glaring daggers at me.

"I don't think your mom likes me."

Jason glanced over his shoulder and shrugged. "Don't take offense. She's like that with everyone." He squeezed my knee gently. "I've known her my whole life and I've seen her smile a handful of times. It's sad. She's very negative."

Dessert arrived, followed by guests dancing. The atmosphere shifted from formal to relaxed and then everyone started having fun. Perhaps it was the wine that flowed easily, making everyone relax. Whether it was the wine, the food, or the conversation, it was working. Even I was dancing in my seat.

Jason removed his tie and folded his shirt sleeves to his elbows. His cheeks had gone rosy as he, too, relaxed. He topped up my wineglass, leaned forward, and kissed my cheek.

"Thank you for coming," he said. "You've made my evening enjoyable." A hand grabbed his shoulder, making him flinch. His mother whispered in his ear. "I'll be right back," he said, squeezing my leg. "Mom just needs to talk business quickly before she leaves," he whispered in my ear.

I leaned back in the chair, watching him walk with his mother to the side of the hall where their voices were drowned out by the music playing. I sipped the wine; it was fruity, with hints of pepper, blackcurrant, and plum, trying to make out what she was saying to Jason.

She possessively squeezed Jason's shoulder, glanced my way, and disappeared down a different corridor. He returned, sitting down with a sigh. The lines between his brows had deepened and his pink cheeks had paled.

"Are you okay?"

He rubbed his face. "Mother is getting married to the new guy," he glanced up and stared at a man who was already staring at us. "He thinks because he's injecting capital into the business, he can do what he wants and tell us how to do it." He turned to face me. "I don't want to talk about it anymore. I hate this place right now. You wanna get out of here?"

"Sure," I said, reaching for my bag.

Jason held my hand as he led us out the back and into the vineyard. There was a building towards the far end of the path. The moon was out, shining on the river, running alongside the vineyard, leaving its silver tendrils flowing over watery rocks. Stridulating insects were on my right, and a cat meowing somewhere nearby.

"This was our first house," Jason said, opening the front door. "It's become my place of escape when I need it, and lately it's often."

"Must you work in the family business?"

He switched on a lamp, bathing the living area in a gentle orange glow, and turned on the stereo; a soft melody filling the space between us.

"They've groomed me to be who they want me to become. I know nothing else. What would I do if I left and where would I go?" He shrugged. His expression told me everything; he felt trapped with nowhere to go.

"Maybe that's what you need to figure out. What do you want to do with your life? Have you ever sat down and really thought about it?"

He stared at me like I sprouted horns.

"I think I need to think long and hard about my future." He stared out of the window overlooking the large estate and the lights flashing from the party. "I need to do this for my sanity or I'm going to die young. I can feel it." He rubbed his chest, and his tone filled with sadness and determination.

"Okay," I said, wanting to change the subject before it became a pity-party. Things had gone depressing quickly, and I wanted the rest of the evening to be happy. "Do you have anything here for us to drink?"

His smile reached his eyes. "Champagne?"

"Yummy."

"I'll be right back." He disappeared down a dark passage.

I settled on the couch near the fireplace. After a couple of minutes and he hadn't returned, I stood up, and stacked some firewood in the fireplace, and lit it. It wasn't cold outside, but having a fire burning now would create a stunning ambiance we needed.

"Much better," Jason said, making me flinch. "I had to search for the bottle in the fridge downstairs." He handed me a glass filled with champagne. "Cheers." We clinked glasses.

Jason held heat in his green eyes as fire reflected in them; and I didn't think it was just the fire making him like that. He placed his glass on the mantlepiece and approached, reaching for me. I set my glass down beside his. His hands cupped my face, and he leaned in.

My hands found his chest. His lips touched mine. The kiss was full of desperation. Our teeth bumped, then once we found our rhythm, the kiss was smooth and lovely. I'd had a few awful kissing partners in my life, but Jason definitely wasn't one of them.

One moment we were standing, the next we were naked on blankets near the fireplace. He'd sheathed his cock with a condom and was thrusting inside of me. Everything had happened so fast I barely had time to register what had happened as I laid beneath him, my hands all over him, him on top of me, and enjoyed the sensations.

When he came, he almost fell on top of me. Sweat peppered his forehead and his skin was damp. He pulled me into the curve of his body as we caught our breaths.

"Sorry," he said, kissing my shoulder blade. "I'll make you cum in a few minutes." He chuckled. "I recover quickly."

Unless he had a vibrator on him, I doubted I could come a second time in one evening, but I didn't want to say that out loud and ruin the moment. Instead, I snuggled into his front.

"Doesn't matter," I said, playing it cool. "The evening has been perfect."

He kissed my shoulder again. We settled into a lovely rhythm of breathing in time and enjoying the warm kisses from the fire. An owl hooted outside, followed by leaves rustling and scraping against the windows.

I flinched when a loud bang sounded from somewhere in front, followed by a door slamming.

"I thought I might find you two here," Hugo said, stomping inside the room. "Mind if I join?" He tripped over his feet, almost slamming into the kitchen counter. He stayed upright and leaned his hip against the counter, folding his arms across his chest.

I pulled Jason's shirt across my naked body and turned around, using his body as a shield.

"What are you doing here?" Jason said.

"Didn't she tell you?" Hugo swung my panties around his finger.

"What?" Jason asked, glancing between the two of us.

"We had some fun in the bathrooms earlier." He thumbed behind him.

Anger flooded my veins. My cheeks heated. I opened my mouth to moan at him when Jason's hand moved over my hips reassuringly.

"I already knew," Jason said with a sigh. "It was obvious when she returned from using the bathroom."

My brows scrunched together.

Jason sat up and turned so he could see us both without craning his neck. "I didn't give you the signal," he said, staring at Hugo.

What? I sat up; the shirt falling to the carpet. I cared little about being naked at this moment.

"We always do this," Hugo said, shrugging and sitting on the couch nearest to us. He stared at me, grinning.

What was going on?

"I haven't spoken to her yet." Jason sounded angry and agitated.

"Ah, but I don't think she'd mind." Hugo winked.

"What is going on?" I said, almost yelling.

Jason let out a deep sigh. "Hugo is actually my step-father," he said, glaring at Hugo. "He introduced me to BDSM when I was twenty, and sometimes we share the same girl." He turned to look at me.

"What?" I stared at Jason, then at Hugo. "You mean you guys tag-team the girl?" I was angry, disgusted, and felt used, but there was another emotion that started to rise above the negative feelings.

"Always with consent," Hugo said, raising his hands in mock surrender. "We don't hurt or harm. It's a fun experience for everyone, especially for the lady."

I stared at them for a moment, unable to find my words. I thought about what they were truly saying.

"What experience are we talking about here, exactly?" I asked, squeezing Jason's shirt tightly against my body.

"Whatever the girl wants to experience," Jason said, leaning against a single chair with his feet brushing against my knees. "Sex with one of us at a time, or both of us, or nothing but cuddling. Whatever you've fantasized about, but were too afraid to do anything about. If you feel comfortable with us, you'll be able to experience anything you want safely. We never cross boundaries."

I pushed myself up against a chair. My feet barely touching Jason's. Hugo removed his shoes and got comfortable on the couch on my left.

Two men. At the same time. Wow. Okay. This was a first for me. I had always wondered about double penetration, but too embarrassed to ask. It seemed my guardian angels had finally listened to me and provided me with this gift; two men willing to share me.

I burst out laughing. "Sorry," I said, covering my mouth to hide the fact that I was nervous. "This is a first for me." I glanced from *'father'* to *'son'*. "Anything?" I said. A nervousness flooded my senses, making me dizzy with anticipation. Perhaps now was the chance I'd been asking for. I glanced at Hugo and then at Jason.

"Whatever you need," Jason said, crawling towards me. He leaned forward and kissed me chastely. "Everything is discussed upfront. We know it's daunting having two guys at the same time, but I want you to feel safe. We won't hurt you. And if anything makes you uncomfortable, we'll stop."

Jason cupped my face, and gently kissed my cheek, lips, then the other cheek. He sat back, pulling me on top of him. I leaned on my knees, hovering above his waistline, without sitting on him. He reached between us and started playing with my already wet folds.

Hugo came in behind me with a bottle of lube. I swallowed hard. He rubbed lube onto his cock and massaged himself. He stared at me like I was prey the entire time. I shut my eyes tight and exhaled a shaky breath. These two men were about to unleash things on me I'd never experienced before, and as scared as I was, it excited me more.

"Kiss me," Jason said, pulling me out of my thoughts.

I leaned forward and planted my lips on his while he fingered me. Hugo rubbed my left ass cheek and slowly pushed a lubed finger inside my ass. I relaxed, allowing him entrance.

Jason grabbed my hip and shifted me in place

above his cock. I sat up and slowly sat down. His hard cock filling me. He leaned further back, taking me with him.

The wet slapping sounds continued behind me as Hugo lathered his cock with lube. He got into position behind me, spreading my ass cheeks open so he could enter me.

"Breathe," Hugo said near my ear, and pushed the tip of his cock inside. I relaxed, pushing slightly into him for easier access.

Jason moved up and down, thrusting gently inside of me to relax me. I gripped his shoulders, my breasts flat against his chest, and exhaled as Hugo entered me. Slowly, an inch at a time, he pushed his cock inside my dark passage, filling me completely.

Once Hugo was balls deep inside my ass, and Jason snuggly inside my pussy, I could only keep still and allowed them to move. They seemed to have a system in place already and knew when to move.

Jason thrusted his hips in short bursts while Hugo had long, deep strokes. They filled me at the same time, leaving me slightly, then filling me again. Over and over, they continued pleasuring my holes, sending sharp bolts of pleasure rippling through my body.

Pressure built. My sensitive ass and pussy their playground. I moved my right hand between Jason and me and rubbed my clit. The moment I did that, I clenched both holes, making both men moan with satisfaction.

"Fuck," Hugo grunted. "Do that again."

I rubbed my clit harder and clenched again.

"Shit," he said, gripping my hips. "You keep doing that, I'm going to cum sooner than I wanted."

A smirk crossed my face, and I rubbed harder, clenching hard again.

"Argh," Hugo groaned and started pounding into my ass. "I'm going to stretch this tight ass of yours."

Jason gripped my hips and slammed into me as much as he could. I was leaning more on my knees than on Jason, affording him the space to move beneath me. I rubbed my clit and clenched. Jason moaned, fighting not to cum. Hugo thrusted harder and harder, the sensations making my body float.

My eyes closed; I enjoyed their touch on and in my body. My mind drifted off to a quiet place where I could simply be. I had no responsibilities to take care of, nothing I had to think about and decide on; I could just enjoy myself as my body released all the feel-good-hormones.

I continued rubbing my clit and clenched. My orgasm smashed into me so violently the men moaned, too. I milked both their cocks as the waves of pleasure moved through my body until finally ending, making my limbs shake.

I fell on top of Jason's chest, exhausted. My heart thundered in my ears and my skin was sticky. Hugo slowly left my body. I coughed and mistakenly pushed Jason out of me. I smiled lazily and stayed on Jason's chest.

Jason moved with me on his chest so that we were both on our sides. He kissed my cheek. "You okay?" He asked tenderly.

"Uh-huh," I mumbled. Still not able to find words to describe what we'd just done. "Yummy," I blurted.

Hugo chuckled. "I think she's completely fucked, but in a good way."

"Definitely," Jason said, rubbing my back. He pulled a blanket over us and hugged me tighter. "You need lots of aftercare after that wonderful experience, and think we need to stay here tonight."

"Okay," I said dreamily, allowing the sandman to take me away.

I awoke the next morning snuggled between two warm bodies. I moved my arms, and they felt heavy and stiff. Then a smile stretched my face in two as I thought about last night; Hugo behind me, Jason beneath me. The motion of their bodies going in and out of mine tightening my core as delicious visions of our evening together flashed before me on repeat. Oh my gods, I could never repeat this to anyone. My cheeks heated.

Hugo stirred on my right, draping his arm over my hips. "Morning, princess," he said, smiling lazily.

"Morning," I said, grinning.

Jason moved on my left, turning around to face me. He cupped my face with his hand and kissed me chastely. "You sleep okay?"

"Yeah, I slept well, thank you." My grin was still on my face and doubted it would disappear anytime soon. "You?" I said, looking at both men.

"Great," Hugo said, stretching.

"Like a rock," Jason said.

"I'll get us breakfast," Hugo said, smacking my ass before getting up and walking naked to the phone in the kitchen.

Jason chuckled and shook his head.

"How did you two get started?" I pointed at Jason, at Hugo, and then at the blankets. "I mean... he's your stepfather... and you are his, you know... how did you two know you liked this?" I stammered, not making sense.

Jason chuckled. "Well, when he and my mom were divorcing I bumped into him and this girl at a pub one night. She was kinky and said she'd love to sleep with him and me. Hugo called me back and asked if I wanted to have some fun." He raised a shoulder. "He told me what he was into and I discovered I enjoyed more than just your average 'vanilla' sex. The rest is history."

I nodded my understanding. "How often do you guys do this?" I said, hoping I wouldn't regret asking this question.

"To be honest, we haven't done it a lot. I think if I had to count, maybe four or five times."

"Okay, you're probably under-counting so that's maybe happened ten times, just to be safe." I laughed.

Jason chuckled, shaking his head. "No, not that many."

"I guess the number of times you've done it doesn't count but that you two play well together."

He glanced at Hugo. "Yeah, we do," he shrugged nonchalantly. "Is it everything you expected it to be?"

"Hmm," I mumbled, the grin still on my face. "My experience was something wonderfully different."

"Glad you enjoyed it. You aren't sore or anything like that?" He asked, caressing my hip.

"I imagined it would've been painful having two cocks inside of me, but it wasn't. I can feel you two were there, but nothing is sore." Silence filled the space for a heartbeat, and I desperately needed to know something. "Would you want to see me again—"

"Of course," Jason said quickly and kissed my forehead. "A proper date with just the two of us. Maybe dinner, some dancing. All that good stuff." His eyes flitted to Hugo, then back to me.

"I hope you aren't trying to exclude me," Hugo said, sitting beside me. "I also want to see this beauty again." He walked his fingers from my hip down to my knees and back again. "My dance moves are better, by the way." He chuckled. "This young man has nothing on me."

"This is so weird," I said, moving on to my back so that they had access to me... if they wanted to continue touching me.

"What?" Jason said.

"Having two men give me attention like you did last night and now. And both of you want to see me again. I've gone years only having first dates with men, a handful went on to two, three, four dates then it sizzled out. And now this. It's surreal."

"You've been going for the wrong types, darling," Hugo said, leaning forward and kissing me. "Breakfast should be here in twenty."

"We have to communicate clearly and properly," Jason said, staring at Hugo. "If we're both going to see her, we need to do this right."

"I know," Hugo said seriously. "I don't want a mess like Sharon again."

"What happened to Sharon?" I asked. My interest piqued.

The men stared knowingly at each other.

"Let's just say she couldn't wait to leave us," Jason added.

My frown deepened.

"We confused her," Jason continued. "Sometimes we'd arrange a date with her on the same day, forcing her to choose between us. Or we'd skip days leaving her alone for two or three days. We were finding our feet in a new dynamic and we kinda fucked up—"

"I don't want to do that again," Hugo said.

"Neither do I," Jason said, glancing my way with a kind smile. "I want to keep this one around for a bit." He winked. "I kinda like her."

"Oh definitely," Hugo said. "Besides, I think this one will nudge us before we fuck up."

I laughed. "Yeah, probably."

When breakfast arrived, we ate at the kitchen table. I wore Hugo's white shirt, savoring the smell of him against my skin. The men wore nothing. Every now and then they'd each touch me; either my arm or leg or lean closer to kiss me. I felt like the luckiest girl in the world, receiving attention from two men I was not only attracted to, but actually wanted to spend time with. And the best part, they wanted to be with and get to know me, too.

I pinched myself.

"Why'd you do that?" Jason asked.

"Pinch myself?"

"Yeah."

"Just making sure I'm not having a wet dream. I mean," I pointed at them, "look at you two. I still can't believe last night happened."

"I know," Hugo said, wiggling his eyebrows. "It was wonderful and I want to do it again, and again, and again." He cupped his dick. "And that clenching. Priceless."

"Haha," I laughed.

"Down, boy," Jason said, patting Hugo's chest. "Baby steps, remember. We can't go love-bombing her so soon or she'll disappear."

"We'll make it work," Hugo said with a head nod.

We finished breakfast and headed for the shower. I wanted this to last and so did the men. We shared the latest STI test results and when we had done them. Once we were content nobody would spread anything and that we'd be monogamous within our dynamic, we wouldn't use condoms anymore.

Hugo pulled me in, his cock pressing against my ass. "I'll be stretching this all by myself some time." He kissed my neck and turned me around. His lips finding mine.

Jason washed himself and then turned those soapy

hands on my back and ass, washing every part of me. He'd finger me while Hugo kissed me and played with my breasts.

I smiled in the kiss as both men played with my body; each had their own way of doing things, the tender caresses, skillful hands, and earth shattering kisses.

Hugo ended the kiss and turned me around, pushing me against Jason. While Jason kissed down my neck, Hugo played with my wet pussy and dark passage while kissing my back.

The sensations were overwhelming, yet I reveled in them. I kissed them, touched them, wanting more from them. I doubled over and sucked Jason's cock while Hugo played with my ass and pussy. Then I'd move to Hugo's cock while Jason played with me. We showered for two hours. By the time we were out and dry, I was exhausted and hungry again. Having two men in my life was bound to make me lose the weight I'd been desperately trying to get rid of.

"I have to go home," I said, pulling on my clothing. "This has been a wonderful time spent with you."

"Who would you like to see first?" Hugo said, folding his sleeves up to his elbows.

"Don't make me choose, please," I said with pleading eyes. I didn't want to do that.

Jason slapped Hugo's chest. "We'll decide, babe,

don't worry. I'll call you later." He closed the distance and kissed me. "And I'll give you the arrangements for tomorrow. I do, however, think you need to rest." He grinned. "I think we've done enough *damage* for today."

"Haha, true, I'm tired and have a few things I need to do today." I couldn't wait to tell Julie about last night, and after that, I'd be on the couch for the rest of the evening, recovering. The muscles in my legs and bum were already stiff.

"I'll get your number from my stepson," Hugo said, slapping Jason's chest. "We'll talk, I promise." He kissed me.

"I need to go before we get naked again and I honestly don't think my body can handle it so soon," I said, picking up my bag. "Chat later. I'm looking forward to our exciting adventures."

I slung my bag over my shoulder and headed for the front door. I glanced behind me at the two men staring back at me, and my heart swelled. This was going to be one of the best adventures ever.

The Cougar in Me

TODD & SANDY

He's tall, had long, curly, dark hair, and a body you could bounce a coin on. He was any woman's wet dream. The problem, he was twenty-two years old. Being a forty-five-year-old woman reaching her peak sexually, I was stuck between a rock and a very hard body; a very sexy, hard body. He was half my age. I felt like one of those sixty-year-old lecherous men preying on young girls fresh out of their parents' home. It was disgusting, but part of today's society.

Todd's profile had a lot of pictures of his body and cock; his very thick and long cock. I blushed each time I browsed through his catalogue. It felt like I was doing online shopping, ready to select an item for purchase.

My phone pinged.

It was a message from Todd; he was the one who'd

initiated contact with me and was adamant about chatting even though we had a twenty-year age gap. He insisted on taking me out on a proper date, which included pre-drinks, dinner, and a walk on Strand beach.

He was sweet, and sexy, and absolutely fuckable, but...

"He's much too young," Eugenie said, curling her hair around her finger. "Way too young." She arched a perfectly styled eyebrow.

I closed the photos of him and pocketed my phone. "There's nothing wrong with going on a date with him. It doesn't mean I'm going to do anything else."

She arched both eyebrows. "Sandy." She'd never said my name like that before. Which told me I'd irritated her or it was the subject; probably both. "He's half your age, girl. He's the same age as your son. How would you feel if a woman your age slept with your little boy?"

"I'm not sleeping with him," I said.

"Yet," she said. Her word dripping with disdain.

I pursed my lips. A cold, sinking feeling settled in my bones. If I was honest with myself, I'd hate it if a woman my age dated my son. I'd want to know what her intentions were. Then I'd smack my son for even entertaining the idea.

I exhaled a frustrated breath. Although it was just a date, and I wasn't going to sleep with him, she was right.

"I can't—"

"Exactly," she said, finishing her sandwich. "It's not right."

"How's hubby?" I asked, quickly changing the subject. As much as I loved her as a friend, I needed some space to think about this without her judging me. She already hated that I was on this kink site, browsing the sea of bodies on offer like a sushi platter.

"He's only coming back next month," she said, but it sounded more like a grumble.

"You don't sound happy."

"No, every time he's home, we fight. I'd rather he stayed there."

Eugenie's husband worked as a pilot in Dubai and came home once a month for a week. Every time he was home, Eugenie came to my house to complain.

"Why don't you just get a divorce?"

The shock on her face was enough to shut me up.

"And then what? I'm on sites like you getting hit on by babies. Gross. No thanks."

"Isn't it better to be on your own than married and miserable?" I'd divorced my husband two years ago, and it was the best thing for both of us. Our son was happier and my ex started dating again and I was genuinely happy for him. I had nothing but love for him and wished him the best. We simply couldn't live together any longer.

Eugenie was stubborn, and afraid of being alone. She was co-dependent on her husband, even though she fought with him constantly. The poor guy, no wonder he was working in Dubai.

"I'm not strong like you."

My eyes widened. It was the first time she admitted something like this to me. Usually she was so guarded and put on a brave face for everything. "You don't know that until you try." I shrugged. "You could surprise yourself."

Her eyes glistened with moisture. "I'm too comfortable."

Our conversation didn't last long after that and we set a date for our next get-together in a month's time. I loved her dearly. She was a good friend, but sometimes she frustrated me so much that I welcomed the distance between us. I simply couldn't reason with her. She listened to answer, not to understand.

When I got home, I had two unread messages from Todd.

> Are we set for tomorrow night?
>
> I'll come and fetch you

I groaned inwardly, not knowing what to do. I wanted to meet him, didn't want to meet him. Perhaps I should just ghost him, block him, but then I'd feel bad for doing that. I still had manners and thought it rude doing such things. As much as it bothered me I was older than him, he genuinely seemed like someone I wanted to be friends with. Perhaps I could meet him and we'd just be friends. Surely that's possible in today's world?

> I'll meet you there

I wrote instead. That way, I could leave when I wanted and didn't have to count on him. I understood he wanted to treat me well, but this was our first encounter and in today's world, a woman couldn't be too safe; even though he was half my age, he was still a male who was twice my size and much stronger.

> See you tomorrow 😉

> I'm looking forward to meeting you

> Me, too

BLAIRE LITTLE

I arrived at the golf course and putt-putt in Stellenbosch on time, and found a parking spot right in front of the restaurant. A car door slammed nearby and a tall man with his hair in a loose bun climbed out of a sleek black Mercedes. His smile reached his eyes when he saw me.

"You're looking ravishing," he said, sauntering over.

This young man was sex on a stick. The hairs on my arms pebbled. I smelled his cologne before he even reached me. He was more good looking in real life than in his pictures. His square jaw ticked and his nostrils flared the closer he got to me.

Fuck me! I hoped I wouldn't cross that invisible '*friend*' line I'd drawn, because right now the '*dynamic/relationship*' one was blinking in neon lights, pulling me towards it like a bee to honey.

"Hi," I said, rocking onto my toes to hug him. He was tall and his pec muscles flexed beneath my breasts. I smiled.

"Hey there," he said, enveloping me with his body, making me feel small, yet protected. He moved his large hands to my waist and squeezed.

I thought his cologne would've been stronger being closer to him, but now I hardly smelled it.

He pulled me against him, taking my breath away. I let go of his neck and pushed lightly against him so he'd let go. He obliged, yet his touch lingered.

Glancing at myself in the car window, I suddenly felt self-conscious. I was mid-forty, had more weight around the middle and hips than I should, and with a wrinkle or two that had formed overnight around my eyes. Strands of silver glistened, making me wish I'd seen the hairdresser before agreeing to this date. I groaned inwardly. I should've put more effort in, but it's not like I was trying to attract him.

Todd leaned closer and kissed my cheek. "Ready for a game of putt-putt?"

"Yes, let's have some fun." I shook the thoughts away; it was only *one* game *and* dinner.

Todd reached for my hand and squeezed it tightly in his. I followed closely behind him with my hand in his. This was our first time meeting and him getting handsy was a bit too soon for me, but I didn't want to let go. It was comforting having him lead the way and taking me with him. I loved it when the man took control of the situation and of me; that was the point of moving away from '*vanilla*' relationships to kink.

"Ladies first," Todd said, standing on one side for me to take the first shot. "I want to watch you move as you swing," he added with a wicked wink.

I wiggled my bum and took the first shot. The ball struck the side, hit the other side, rolled over the hole, and struck the windmill. "Dammit," I grumbled and stomped towards my ball, pushing it into the hole.

"Two for you," he said, scribbling on the score sheet. "My turn," he said with a naughty smirk.

Todd made a show of wiggling his bum as I did, held the club wrong, and hit it where I did, also getting two points.

My eyes narrowed. *What was he up to?*

At the next hole, Todd hit the ball exactly where I did, and getting the same score; 3. The same thing happened at the next one and the next.

"Why are you following me?" I asked jokingly at hole 5.

"Because, my dear, where you go, I follow."

That was the most romantic line, the cheesiest, or the creepiest. A woman could never be too careful these days, but Todd didn't give me the creepy vibes like I'd experienced when a true creep creeped me out.

"That means nobody wins."

He nodded. "Your turn."

The rest of the game was the same and at the end of the game, we both had fifty-five points.

"Now what?" I said dramatically with a wave of my arms. "We both win." I smiled.

"Exactly, that means we both get ice cream after dinner."

We walked to the restaurant next door to the putt-

putt where the server took us to the table he'd booked ahead of time.

"Great table," I said in awe. Our table sat on the covered veranda of the restaurant overlooking the golf course with its dams and flowerbeds. They'd just cut the grass and now that smell hung in the air, reminding me of my childhood.

"I know," he said. "I don't eat here often because I'm always playing out there," he pointed at the golf course, "and when I pass the restaurant, my eyes land on this table in the corner. When I asked you out, I knew I had to book it for us."

"It's lovely. Thank you."

The food was okay, but not worth the cost; I kept that to myself, not wanting Todd to think I was a food snob or didn't appreciate his effort. We finished our meal and after dinner coffee by nine o'clock. When we stood to leave, I noticed we were the only ones left.

"Would you like to go clubbing?" he asked, glancing at his watch.

I stifled a yawn, unable to remember the last time I went clubbing. It was nine o'clock at night; I usually went to bed soon thereafter, and as much as I'd love to go home now and sleep, I didn't want to act my age. Besides, it was much too early to go to bed on a Saturday evening. I might enjoy it.

"Sure, why not?" I shrugged.

"Would you like to drop your car off at home? We'll be heading to Cape Town."

"Oh," I said, and all the energy I had seeped out of my bones. We'd get there by ten, leave maybe at twelve, home after one. I wasn't so sure I wanted to still go, but this didn't happen often. *Why not?* "Okay, that makes sense."

We arrived at the club a few minutes after ten. I was told I had too much clothing on and had to remove my top. I felt awkward wearing my black bra and pulled my jacket closed.

Todd held my hand as we navigated through the sea of moving bodies who wore even less clothing than me.

"What kind of party is this?" I asked, staring at a couple who only had the bare essentials covered with leather straps.

"It's a kink party."

I mumbled '*oh*' as my eyes bounced from one person to the next; a girl wearing fishnet stockings, a g-string, and nipple caps; a boy in hot pants and a harness being pulled by his mistress who wore a sexy black teddy; a girl with white hair and white straps covering the important parts reminding me of *The Fifth Element* movie. When she turned her back on me, she had tiny white wings stuck to the straps near her shoulder blades; she looked ethereal.

"Would you like a drink?" Todd asked.

I nodded. I might as well enjoy the club since I was already here.

I flinched when someone grabbed my shoulders to reach Todd. Todd spun around to ask me what was wrong when he saw the other person and his cheerful expression dropped. I turned to see who the arm belonged to, coming face to breasts with a tall woman strong enough to punch my lights out.

Todd's eyes flitted from me to the woman.

"Todd," she said. Every emotion emphasized in that one word; his name. It told me she was angry, bitter, and possibly spiteful. She arched an eyebrow at me, like I was gum at the bottom of her shoe, then looked at Todd again. It was obvious she thought I was beneath her.

"Guinevere, what are you doing here?"

"When I heard you were on your way here with someone, I had to see myself whether it was true. Who in their right mind would come to a kink party with someone like you is beyond me."

A hollow, sinking feeling struck the pit of my stomach. I didn't like where this was going.

"I hurt no one. You know this. Whoever is spreading these vicious rumors needs to come and tell me what their issue is with me to my face." He stared at Guinevere with such intensity it made me uncomfortable and step backwards. Todd sensed this and pulled me closer to his side. His grip on me tightening.

Guinevere glowered down at me. She was as tall as Todd, muscular, yet looked petite. It was the scowl on her face that made her ugly.

"Well," she shrugged, "you should've thought about that before dumping me."

Todd exhaled a frustrated breath. "We weren't compatible, we don't like the same kinks, we had sex once, and then you became possessive of me. You freaked me out. You need two lovers to keep you busy, because one isn't enough for you. The sooner you realize I'm not the one for you, the better for you. I think it's time you move on from me."

Guinevere stood tall even though her shoulders slumped forwards ever so slightly. She blinked unshed tears. She liked him; a lot. She may even have had feelings for him that were conveniently squashed after those words he spewed. They were hurtful, but she seemed to be someone you needed to be very direct with or she wouldn't understand.

"I'm sorry," Todd continued. "But you really need to forget about me. There are others here who are better suited for you. I've met someone now. Please respect my decision."

Guinevere closed her eyes as if trying to calm

down. When she opened them again, tears threatened to burst. "Okay," she said, glancing at me and nodded. "Okay, I accept that you've met someone else. It hurts. I thought we had a connection. Had something. But I see now it was one-sided."

"Hey, babe," a guy said, snaking his arms around Guinevere's middle. "Where did you disappear to?" He glanced at us. "Who are they?"

"Just friends," she said, putting on a fake smile, but I could tell she was deeply hurt.

"Im Jono," he said, sticking his hand out for us to shake. "Come babe, everyone is waiting for us." He let her go and reached for her hand. "Bye guys, you're welcome to join us in the back. We're about to smoke some weed."

"We're good, thanks," Todd said.

"You snooze you lose," Jono shrugged, pulling Guinevere behind him.

Guinevere glanced over her shoulder at Todd and when she turned to face the way she was going, I got a sense she would rather be with Todd.

"Explain," I said with kindness. "If you want." I smiled.

"We dated briefly and when I broke it off, she didn't take it well. I tried to be gentle, but I failed. So I had to be harsh now. I hate speaking to someone like that, but she wasn't getting it, you know. I'm not that person; it's mean."

"Okay, I understand," I said. "Are there any other women I need to know about?"

He chuckled. "No, babe, it's just you. If you still want me?"

Did I want him? Did I really want to do this? Something within me screamed *yes.*

"I'm still thinking about things," I said, grinning.

He pulled me in for a hug. "Let's get that drink I promised."

We danced, enjoyed one drink, and laughed. I saw many outfits that intrigued me and would love to wear. Todd shared with me which outfits he wanted me to wear for him, making me nervous yet excited.

The entire time we were there, not once did he come across as someone half my age. His maturity was beyond his age, making me feel younger than I was. I loved it and although at first I didn't want to pursue anything with him; I was now open to the idea.

Todd dropped me off at home just before two in the morning and promised to be back around lunchtime. There was a picnic with our name on and I had to attend. I couldn't help but smile. He wasn't shy to show he cared, was into me, and more importantly, he didn't play games.

I was ready by one o'clock. He arrived a minute past. As he knocked, I opened the door. We both wore smiles that lit our eyes.

"You ready?" he asked.

"Yes," I grabbed my sun hat and bag, "let's go."

He took us to a wine estate in Stellenbosch. The gardens circled around a dam where ducks and ducklings swam. There were willow trees to picnic under and one section where younger kids could play on wooden jungle gyms.

"I've ordered a picnic basket that has a bit of everything," Todd said as we walked hand-in-hand towards the restaurant.

I waited on one side while he fetched the basket from the collections window.

"Let's go." He grabbed my hand and handed me the blanket while he carried the basket. "How about we sit over there," he pointed towards the far end of the garden across the dam. It was the furthest from everywhere.

"Okay," I said, feeling excited for something, but didn't know what. My smile kept stretching my face in two and I was glad he couldn't see me; I was sure I looked silly.

We passed another couple enjoying their picnic when I stopped and removed my sandals. "There, grass to ground me."

Todd kicked off his flip-flops and undid the top two buttons of his shirt, revealing more of his chest. I tried not to stare, but it was difficult.

We arrived at our secluded section of the garden where a leafy fence sheltered us from the vineyard behind us, trees protected us from the side, and a couple of bushes lined the dam. We were in a room grown with love from nature all to ourselves.

"How did you know about this area?" I asked, grinning. At first glance, this section looked like a garden, but because of its proximity from the rest of the wine estate nobody came this side.

He chuckled, and it sounded wonderful. He placed the picnic basket on the grass and helped me open the blanket for us to sit on.

"I was here for a private function last year and booked it for today. Thought we could use the privacy... to talk."

I didn't want to talk. I wanted to do dirty things with this man. The veins in his hands stuck out, and I wondered what his fingers felt like around my throat, squeezing my waist, or even between my legs. I bit my bottom lip at the dirty thoughts.

This man was going to drive me crazy with lust, but I also wanted more. I wanted more than just the physical aspect, and based on Todd's way of doing things, I think he wanted that too.

I dropped my sandals a short distance away and started unpacking the items out of the basket; bottle of red wine, two glasses, a bottle of sparkling water, a cheese board, a meat selection, a pasta salad, a packet of sweet potato crisps, a bag of mixed nuts, two chocolate mousse desserts, two bread rolls, two containers of butter, jam, and a handful of chocolate mints.

"Wow," I said, tearing the wrapper on the cheese board and tasting the gouda. "Delicious."

"Haha, let me open the wine," he said, reaching for the bottle. He poured us a generous amount in each glass and handed me one.

"This is lovely," I said, clinking my glass against his. "We have a beautiful view," I pointed at the mountains behind us, and the dam, "we have pleasant weather, delicious food, and splendid company. Thank you."

I'd been married for years and not once did my ex-husband want to go on a picnic with me. He'd said it was boring, and he didn't like spending time outside with the insects or sitting on the grass. Being out here with Todd felt rejuvenating.

"I'm glad you're enjoying it." He placed his wine

glass on a flat spot beside him, opened his shirt completely, and sat back. His shorts fit him perfectly, hugging his muscular legs.

I lifted my dress above my knees so that I could tan my legs a bit. I placed my wine glass beside me, too, and picked at the food.

We ate most of the food. Todd placed the dessert and chocolates to one side for later. He wanted us to finish the wine before having dessert.

When he started packing the empty containers inside the basket, I got up. "No, don't go anywhere. I'm just making space."

"Oh," I said, and started helping him. "What are we doing next?"

He didn't answer me. It was only when the blanket was clean did he look at me. "Lie on your back here," he said, standing, and pointed at the blanket.

I laughed nervously. "Okay." I did as he asked and got comfortable on the blanket.

He removed his shirt and placed it on the top right-hand corner of the blanket near my head. Then he removed his pants. I swallowed hard, torn between two thoughts; relieved he kept his underwear on, but also wanting him to take them off.

He stood over me and stared down with hunger in his eyes. He crouched, then straddled my waist, placing his hands near my head and hovered above me, just staring at me.

The weight of his gaze made me want to look away, but I didn't. I stared back, looking deep into his eyes as he did.

He sat up and grabbed my wrists, pinning them above my head. My breath caught in my throat and my mouth parted. My heart thundered in my chest. He leaned forward, hovering above me, his lips only centimeters away. I felt his hot breath on my face. He closed the gap. I closed my eyes. His lips touched mine. My heart skipped a beat. Wetness pooled between my legs as I felt his hardness press against my front; and he was hard.

His lips were soft, his tongue tasting mine, his need clear. So was my need; I moaned as I tried to touch him, but he gripped my wrists in place. My pelvis tilted upward without me thinking. All I knew was I wanted more of him. I wanted him deep within me.

He ended the kiss, and his nostrils flared. "I've wanted to kiss you since I saw you yesterday," he said. "I'm glad I waited." He smiled. "You're worth it, every inch of you." His eyes found my breasts.

He eased his grip on my wrists, but then he grabbed my elbows and pushed my arms up and straight so that my arms touched my ears. Slowly, he moved down my body. His fingers lightly caressing down my arms and brushing against the sides of my breasts, making my nipples hard. He smiled. His eyes held heat. I grinned. His hands trailed down the curve of my ribs, waist, and then he went back up again. He shifted his body lower down my body so that his hands could caress my hip bones.

"I want to do things to you, but I need to know you're okay with these things."

He stroked my hips over the dress and each time he went over my hip bones, juices flooded between my legs. I wanted to give him access.

I swallowed hard. "Like, what things?"

"Like massages," he said. "Touches, kisses, caresses, and everything in between."

I nodded. "Fine with me."

"What about spanking?"

My cheeks heated. I nodded. I was sure my eyes smiled with excitement.

He leaned forward, bruising my lips with his. I got so caught up in the kiss I moaned as my arms found his body, but he wouldn't have that, and gripped my wrists once more, placing them near my head.

He ended the kiss, sat up, reached for the hem of my dress, and slowly lifted it.

"Mmmm," he said when he noticed I wasn't wearing underwear. "How did I not notice this?" He grinned as I sat up to lift my dress over my head. My breasts spilling free of their soft restrains. "Christ."

I laid back down and stared at him. He glanced around, ensuring nobody was near, and closed the distance once more. Near the shell of my ear, he whispered, "I want to have sex. Is that okay?"

"Uh-huh," I mumbled, nodding. I'd like that. My body heated, yet I shivered.

Todd removed the rest of his clothing, and his cock sprang free. He sheathed his cock with a condom and nestled between my legs. He pressed the tip near my opening and slowly nudged inside. I got comfortable and relaxed. He pushed in deeper. I exhaled. He thrusted in and out a few times before going deeper to give me time to get used to his size.

My body hummed from his pleasurable assault. Every nerve ending sparked, sending a current into my veins, awaking parts of me I once thought had died with my marriage. His kisses were gentle, his hands still gripping my wrists, and his hard body pounding into mine. Everything beautifully coordinated.

"I want you on your hands and knees," he said, exiting me and helping me shift into position. He pressed my head into the blanket, my ass in the air, and pushed my legs apart. "I want to reach deep inside of you," he said as he thrusted into me. It felt as though he was hitting my bellybutton. He smacked my ass cheeks one after the other, making me clench around him, and making him moan each time. After each smack, he'd rubbed the burning area, soothing it.

Todd stopped, grabbed under my left leg, lifted me onto my side, and entered me again.

"Ah," I said, feeling him hit a unique spot. He massaged me internally with his cock. I just got used to that feeling when he hooked the same leg over his arm and I moved onto my back. When he thrusted inside, I didn't think he could go any deeper, but he did.

I sunk into the grass and ground beneath me; my body feeling light as my mind drifted.

When his hand moved between us, my eyes shot open as he played with my clit. He rubbed it hard as he continued pounding into me. I barely had a chance to ask him to slow down when my orgasm struck. I grabbed his wrist and pressed him into me as I milked his cock. He moaned. I shuddered from the waves of pleasure. His co-ordination shifted, and he came, too.

When the orgasm subsided, leaving behind aftershocks, Todd removed his hand and snuggled in behind me. He planted kisses along my shoulder while his fingers caressed down my sides, sending goosebumps all over my body. His hand continued tickling my side, as he kissed my head and neck, making me squeal.

"That's ticklish," I said, trying to squirm out of his grasp.

"Good," he said, chuckling. "I like that sound you make." He kissed my neck again, forcing another squeal out of me.

"Enough," I said, turning around to face him. It was then that I once again noticed he was a twenty-something young man; he had no wrinkles, no gray hairs, nothing letting me know life had scarred him. Not that it was a problem; it told me he still had to experience life even though his behavior and actions were of someone older and wiser.

"What are you thinking about?" he asked, pressing his thumb lightly between my eyebrows. "So much wrinkling going on here."

I was thinking about his age and how much younger he was, but I didn't want to say it. Instead, I raised my eyebrows slightly to remove the wrinkles there, and smiled. "That was wonderful," I said, leaning closer to kiss him. "You are... talented." I grinned.

"I'm glad you had fun," he said. "But I still want to know what you were thinking just now. You don't have to answer me now, but one day soon."

I rolled my eyes.

"What was that? Did you just roll your eyes? That

is disrespectful and requires a bum whack." He stretched his arm and smacked my ass. *Hard*.

"Ow," I moaned, rubbing the area. "That hurt."

"Good," he said, playfully. "Now, I'd like to see you again. I understand during the week can be difficult since we both work. How about next Friday? There's a dungeon I'd like to take you to."

Butterflies flapped their wings inside my stomach. I'd never been to a dungeon before, and thought about all the kinky equipment we could try out. Then I felt sad. *How many women had he taken to this place?* I knew it shouldn't bother me, but it did.

"Your frown is back," he said, rubbing between my eyebrows. "What are you thinking?"

"Nothing—"

"It's not nothing," he said seriously, sitting up and bringing me with him. "Talk to me. Open communication is important to me, and if we're to continue seeing each other, I'd like us to say what's bothering us. And something has bothered you twice already."

"It's stupid."

"Tell me. I want to hear it all."

"I'm forty-five and have had my fair share of experience, but the thought of you taking women to this dungeon didn't sit well with me for a second."

"Okay, that was now. What about before?"

I groaned inwardly. "You're the same age as my son, and you don't even have a wrinkle." I sighed.

"Thank you for sharing those two concerns with me. I appreciate your openness." He smiled kindly and scooted closer to me so that he could touch me. He leaned forward and kissed my cheek. "You will be the second person I'm taking to the dungeon. The first time was with that girl you met last night."

I nodded, feeling relieved.

"Age means nothing to me, and so what if I'm the same age as your son. Maybe one day I can meet him, and it shouldn't bother you either—"

"Are you sure? There are younger girls out there. They have more energy. They're open to trying different things. Don't have trauma," I said, interrupting him.

"One," he said, raising his index finger, "don't interrupt me," he smiled and slapped the top of my hand and quickly kissed it. "Two," he raised the middle finger, "you've been more open and willing than any '*young*' girl I've spoken to. Three," he raised a third finger, "you have more than enough energy for me. Now," he leaned forward and kissed me on the nose. "Stop worrying about younger girls, or any girl for that matter, and definitely stop worrying about our age difference. We like each other and want to continue seeing each other, don't we?"

"Yes," I said, nodding.

"Good," he kissed my hand again. "Let's get dressed before someone catches us naked." He winked. "Or we get sick."

I giggled. He was so demanding, but I loved it when a man took control of the situation and of me. It told me he cared enough to do that; he wanted to be in control instead of sitting back and leaving everything up to me.

We dressed and packed up. We enjoyed a leisurely stroll of the gardens before handing the basket and blanket back to the restaurant.

"I don't want the date to end," Todd said, stopping near the exit. He combed his fingers through my still messy hair. I took that as a hint and neatened it as much as I could. "Let's have a coffee somewhere." He picked a leaf off my shoulder. I laughed.

"Shouldn't we maybe shower and put on fresh clothing?"

"No, I like smelling you on me. I want to be reminded that we were on the grass together. I want us to look like we were naughty." His grin split his face in two. "Come, I know a decent place nearby."

"Okay," I said, walking beside him.

The coffee shop was busy, but we found a spot in a quiet corner. We ordered our coffees and waited for them to arrive before saying a word.

Todd reached for my hand and placed it on his thigh. He sipped his coffee. "I want to be your dominant. Your lover. Your boyfriend. Everything you need."

I scooted closer so I could hear him properly. Our legs touched. It had been so long since I was in a relationship with a man who wanted me to touch him all the time; I had to remind myself to keep my hand there.

I kissed his shoulder. "I'd like that, too, and I'll do my best not to let the age thing bother me since I now understand how you feel about it, and won't stress about it either."

"Good, because it's nothing." He kissed me chastely.

The week flew by. Although work was busy, all I thought about was Todd and our time together at the picnic. We spoke daily, sharing parts of our lives with each other. It was a breath of fresh air being with someone who didn't let his ego get in the way or played games. He was emotionally available and wanted us to be more than just something *physical*.

I was ready and waiting by six o'clock on Friday

afternoon. He knocked on my door five minutes later. I jumped off the couch, almost slamming into the door to open it. He wore dark blue jeans and a tight black top. He'd tied his dark, curly hair in a messy man-bun.

"Darling," he said, kissing me. "You ready?" he asked, smiling when he noticed my clothing.

"Yep," I said happily and reached for my bag.

"So," he said, holding my hand. "What's underneath that coat?" He leaned forward to peek inside, but I swatted his hand away.

"You'll find out when we get there," I said with a naughty giggle.

"Mmmm," he said, narrowing his eyes. "I can't wait to tell you to take it off."

I kept my hand on his leg with his hand on top of mine all the way to the dungeon. We sat in a comfortable silence with music playing in the background.

We arrived at the venue and greeted by the owner, who handed us a basket of goodies. Todd handed me the basket and paid the owner. Inside the basket was lube, chocolates, bottles of water, and crisps; perfect for a day in the kinky dungeon.

We entered the venue, and I wrinkled my nose. "What's that smell."

"Just cleaning agents."

"Smells like a morgue."

"So morbid." He chuckled, shaking his head in

amusement. "Come," he said, I want to tie you to the cross first."

My stomach dropped. "Okay," I said nervously. I placed the basket on the nearby table and glanced around; St Andrews cross, fucking swing in the center, a four-poster bed with loops to secure restraints, a modern bondage spanking bench, a cage in the corner, and a bathroom on one side. "Wow," I said, my eyes bouncing across the various equipment.

"I hope you're excited?"

"I am, but also nervous."

"I'll look after you and if you become overwhelmed with anything, let me know, and I'll stop immediately. Okay? There are no *musts* here."

"Okay," I said, still staring at the equipment.

"Now," he reached for the coat, "I want to see what's underneath this." He undid the buttons, loosened the belt, and opened the coat. He whistled. "Fuck me!" he said. "You're beautiful."

I removed the coat and placed it on top of my bag on the floor. "You want me here?" I said, walking towards the cross.

"Yeah," he said, sounding dreamily. He rubbed his hard cock, but the expression he wore told me he was in pain. "I don't know if I can last." He chuckled. "Being a Dom, you'd think I'd mastered the art of control. But damn, woman, you can't just be naked under that coat and expect me not to be aroused."

"Haha." I turned around when I reached the cross. I leaned against it, tapping my high heel on the floor. "I'm waiting, sir."

"Mmm, so you are." He approached with purpose. "Hands up," he said. His voice was deep and throaty, making my arms pebble.

Wicked Games featuring Parra for Cuva and Anna Naklab played through the speakers. I smiled. This was a favorite song of mine, except I might actually fall in love with Todd if he continued like this. I'd keep that to myself, of course, not knowing if I was just a plaything to him, or if this was real.

I watched him near and raised my hands. He closed the gap and slowly touched my right arm first, and tied my wrist there. Then he did the same on the left arm, caressing lightly up my arm, then fastening me in place.

"Spread your legs," he said, crouching. He tied my ankles to the cross and glanced up at me. His eyes flitted from my face to my open pussy. He groaned. His fingers walked up the inside of my leg. He stood up, but kept his hand between my legs. When he leaned forward, his fingers entered my wet pussy. "So vulnerable, so sexy, so mine," he said near the shell of my ear. He kissed my neck while he finger fucked me.

I pulled on my restraints, wanting to touch him,

but he ensured I couldn't do that. My legs wouldn't close; being spread wide open like that left me feeling completely exposed, but I loved how his fingers entered me over and over; first one finger then two. I leaned my head back and enjoyed the sensations.

He reached for something on the side and switched it on. My eyes shot open, and I glanced down. He stared at me as he moved the device closer to my moist folds. He pressed it against my clit and continued to finger fuck me.

"Please, sir, can I come?" I moaned as my orgasm threatened to smash into me. I squirmed, trying to move away from him, but he'd tied my waist to the cross and I didn't remember him doing that.

He didn't answer me.

"Sir!!" I yelled. "Please, may I come?"

His stare intensified as he pressed the device harder against my clit. "Come for me," he whispered.

The moment he said that, I relaxed. I gave in to the moment, listening to Stephen Sanchez sing **Evangeline**; his lyrics were dreamlike, making me smile sleepily. I allowed the orgasm to sear through my body like lava from a volcano threatening to erupt inside of me. I moaned as the waves struck one after the other. Todd didn't remove the device, making the orgasm continue on and on, and I continued to moan. My eyes rolled into the back of my head. His fingers continued fucking me and I squeezed my pussy around those fingers. A layer of sweat covered my body as the orgasms continued. I wanted him to stop as the pleasurable pain came in with the tide, but I'd lost my voice, rendering my moan silent. Darkness surrounded me; the soft blackness like velvet against my naked skin, sucking me deeper beneath the surface.

When I opened my eyes, I was on the bed, licking dry lips. "Um," I said, licking my lips again.

"Here," Todd said, helping me sit up. "Drink."

My eyes found his, and I opened my mouth to drink the water he offered. "What happened?"

Wildfire, a Colyn remix with Rüfüs Du Sol, played, my foot moving with the beat.

He chuckled. "You, my dear, drifted off so far and so deep. You've been gone for almost an hour."

"What?" I flinched. "That was unbelievable, sir. I felt so much. I... I seemed to have disappeared there. It... it was something else. Um," I stammered, losing my train of thought.

"All that orgasm denial during the week and us teasing constantly finally hit home. I'd like to say that we did a great job today." He leaned forward and kissed my temple.

"Haha. I hope the day isn't over?"

"We can do whatever you feel like doing. Just

remember, your body went through a lot now. We mustn't overdo it. We can always come back."

"It's that Hitachi device you kept on me. Oh, my word..." I smacked dry lips again. Todd handed me the bottle of water and I enjoyed a long sip.

"Your pleasure is my pleasure." He kissed me chastely.

I leaned back on the pillow and closed my eyes, feeling his gaze on me without having to check. "I'd like to try the spanking bench next with my bum up in the air," I opened my eyes to watch his reaction, "so that you can have your way with me, whichever hole you desire. If that's what you want?" I shrugged.

He chuckled. "Absolutely. I'd love to stretch you, and then stretch you." He winked wickedly.

My elbows, knees, and stomach were on the spanking bench and carefully supported. The pads beneath me were soft and comfortable.

Slowly, Todd fastened me to each relevant section of the bench, making sure I couldn't fall off and get hurt. He spanked each ass cheek hard, leaving a burning sensation. He didn't rub my bum. Instead, he approached the far wall and grabbed the flogger.

I exhaled a nervous breath and closed my eyes. I wanted my senses to awaken so that I could feel more than I would've if I watched.

"I'll ask you how you're doing. Okay?"

"Yes, sir," I said, blowing out my breath.

Todd began with whisper soft slaps on my back, bum, and hips. The tapping was soft and hypnotic. One, two across the shoulder blades, three, four across the bum, five, six on the hips. Then he'd start over again. With each cycle, he'd hit harder until each slap stung.

"Color?"

"Orange, sir," I said, breathing through the sting.

"Last round. I don't want you going too deep again." He rubbed my left ass cheek. His thumb making its way to my dripping and swollen pussy. The song **Bellyache** from Billie Ellish played over the speakers. I moved my bum along with the beat. "Keep still," he whacked my bum hard, and chuckled.

I grinned, keeping my body still.

"Good girl."

That word; *good girl* always did something to me. Although I was forty-five, being called a *good girl* turned me into a blubbering mess, putty in his hands, to do with as he pleased.

"I'm going to stretch your pussy, and then your tight dark hole." Todd rubbed the dark passage, inserting a lubed finger. "That's it, relax for me." He continued stretching my ass so that I could handle his cock. "I don't want to hurt you. I want to pleasure you." He pushed two fingers from his other hand into my pussy and thrusted into both holes at the same time. "And I want to cum inside your ass. Is that okay with you?"

"Mmm, yes, sir."

His fingers going in and out of me were wonderful. I gripped the bench, and relaxed my body. I gave in to him and the sensations he unleashed within me. **Rise** from Lynnic played; their tune hypnotic, sending me into a trance and deeper into my sub-space.

Todd moved behind me, water ran and splashed, and he was back. He touched my hips with his cold, wet hands as he pushed his hard cock into my pussy. "Oh gods," he said, slipping deeper into me. "You're so swollen inside. Fuck me."

I grinned, doubting he'd last long enough to stretch my ass, but we'd see how things went.

I clenched around him as he pounded into me. The bench squeaking slightly. His grip tightened on my hips. The flesh slapping flesh echoed around us each time he went deeper.

"Aaah," he moaned and stopped, pulling out. "Fuck me," he said, chuckling. "I almost came there." Something clicked and squirted. "I want this ass, though." He moved behind me. "I'm pushing your vibrator in, and then my cock in your ass."

"Yes, sir," I said, drifting further away. After all those orgasms, I wasn't sure I could orgasm again, but

I'd see. My body was alive from his touch and bound to burst into flames.

Slowly, he inserted the vibrator and switched it on. **Who are you** from mehro played. The song was calm and delicate, and I relaxed as Todd pushed his cock inside my ass. The vibrator fit snuggly and even more so as Todd pushed more of himself into me, and started pounding into my ass.

The little arm of the vibrator struck my clit at the right spot with each thrust, sending sparks all over my body. Every time Todd slammed into me, he pushed the vibrator deeper inside, and the little arm hit my clit harder. Over and over, deeper and deeper, he pounded into me.

"Sir!" I yelled. "I'm going to cum." I didn't think it was possible, but it was about to happen. *Again.*

"Cum for me," Todd grunted through clenched teeth. It sounded like he was fighting his orgasm, and the moment I moaned, he slowed his movements as his orgasm struck. He kept his cock inside of me until he emptied his ball sack. I clenched around him and the vibrator. He moaned again. "Christ," he mumbled and slowly exited, taking the vibrator with him.

Water splashed. He returned and cleaned me with warm water and a face cloth before releasing me from my restraints.

"That was the first time feeling the vibrator like that," he said.

I didn't need to look at him to know he was smiling.

"That was unbelievable," he added, freeing me and helping me stand on shaky legs. "I think we need a shower."

I hugged him. His wet chest against my face was comforting as he held me close. We walked together towards the shower area. He tested the water first and helped me inside. He washed me first, then himself. I leaned against the tiles for support, watching him.

Let's fall in love for the night, by FINNEAS echoed around us. Todd got us towels, wrapped one around me first before himself. Then he helped me walk to the bed.

I climbed onto the bed half wet and collapsed on top of it, with Todd climbing in behind me.

The next Friday, Todd arranged to fetch me at home for date night. When seven o'clock came and went, I phoned him, but it went straight to voicemail. An hour passed, and I was worried something had happened to him. I phoned again, but it went straight to voicemail.

I made myself a cup of tea to stop myself from overthinking something had happened, but it didn't help. I was worried; I overthought all possible scenarios. *Was he in an accident? Did he find someone else? Did he leave me? Was he in hospital?*

Unfortunately, past traumas always found their way to the surface no matter how long I tried to heal from them. I exhaled a breath and shook out the silly thoughts. *Nothing was wrong, he was just delayed.*

My phone pinged.

> Are you sure this is the man you want?

The message was from an unknown number. The lines between my eyes deepened.

> Who is this?

<<picture sent>>

The picture was of Todd and Genevieve. They were having sex on Todd's bed. The date and time stamp were fifteen minutes ago.

My veins filled with ice, my palms became clammy, and a headache blossomed.

> **What's going on?**

> Todd isn't who he says he is. I thought I'd share this with you before you became attached to a lying, cheating, scum bag like him!!!!!

I phoned Todd's cell, and it rang for a long time before he answered.

"Hello?" he eventually said, sounding confused.

"Todd?"

"Yeah, who's this?"

"It's me, Sandy."

"Crap, Sandy. We had a date tonight, didn't we? What time is it? My head," he stammered, knocking things over. There were hushed sounds in the background, followed by movement.

"Is it true? That you're there with Genevieve?"

"It's not what you think," he said. *"It's not me."*

"Did you just sleep with her?" I yelled, fighting to keep the tears at bay.

"It wasn't me. You must believe me. She came around to fetch some of her stuff and then... she offered me juice," he smacked his lips together, *"I don't know what's going on."* There was silence. *"Genevieve! What the fuck did you give me?"* He yelled. *"Why is there a*

metallic taste in my mouth? And what the fuck is all this..."

I pinched my eyes shut. What the...? I couldn't finish the sentence. *What happened over there? What did Genevieve do to him?*

My heart slammed against my ribs, hoping this was a mistake, that Todd didn't do this on purpose. That he wasn't lying and messing me around.

"Todd?"

After a moment of him screaming in the background, I yelled to get his attention.

"Babe? Fucking hell. I need to get my blood tested or something. She drugged me. Can you come fetch me? I don't think I can drive."

"Where is Genevieve?"

"I kicked her out. I didn't want her near me." The tone of his voice made me scared for him.

"I'm on my way."

"We'll know more once your results come back," the doctor said after drawing blood from Todd. "From what you've told me, here's a course of antibiotics. I'll also do a full STI screening and HIV test. I'll give you my findings to take to the police."

"Thank you, doctor," Todd said. He had paled, and his bloodshot eyes were red-rimmed like he'd been crying all evening. He had cuts and bruises all over his body, like Genevieve had beat him with a stick.

"Do you remember anything?" the doctor asked.

Todd shook his head. "I don't want to remember what she did to me," he said ominously. "I just don't want any nasties." He glanced at me with tears welling in his eyes.

I stood closer to him, wrapping my arms around his shoulders, and kissed his cheek. "Everything isn't okay now, but it will get better." I didn't know what else to say. Genevieve had sexually assaulted and drugged him. Nobody should go through something like that. I just hoped it didn't leave a lingering scar on him that affected who he was going forward; not that I would run away. I hoped he didn't push me away for anything he might fear.

Todd pulled me closer, pressing his head on my breasts. Boobs; they made everything better. I smiled and kissed the top of his head.

"Everything will be okay once I hear back with the results." Todd glanced at the doctor. "Is there anything else I can take just in case?"

"No, the antibiotics is a broad spectrum that will

rid most STIs." He stared with compassion in his eyes. "I should get the results tomorrow."

I drove Todd back to his place after laying charges at the police station. They took pictures of his body and made copies of the doctor's report. I also sent them the picture of Genevieve and Todd she'd sent me; the more I looked at it, the more disturbed I felt. I could tell Todd wasn't really partaking in the sinful act. She was on top of him, his arms were wide like he'd fallen on the bed, and she was riding him.

I bit back tears. I needed to be strong for him.

"It's okay," he said, kissing my forehead. "This is shit, but I don't need you to be strong for me. I can see this is bothering you."

"I know you'll be okay, and we'll be okay, but I hate what she did to you. And now all I want to do is take care of you." I dabbed antibacterial cream on a cut on his shoulder.

"No, babe," he reached for my hand and kissed the top. "I know your motherly instincts are kicking in, but I'm here to look after you. You're MY sub, I'm YOUR Dom. I don't want you to mother me, okay?" The intensity in his gaze made me feel like I did something wrong.

"We're just looking after each other."

"I know," he said, "but I'll tell you want I want. I don't want you topping from the bottom and do what you think I want. Okay?" He kissed my temple. "Now, clean my wounds." He winked and leaned back. "Clean, kiss, clean kiss."

I smiled. Now I understood what he meant. This was going to take some getting used but, I now knew what he wanted. "Yes, sir," I said, kissing him chastely.

After I cleaned a wound, I kissed beside it until every cut and bruise was taken care of.

Todd's cellphone chimed. "They've arrested Genevieve, and she confessed," he said after reading the text. "They're charging her with aggravated assault, rape, and attempted murder."

"Jeez, hectic."

"Good. She needs to get off the streets and get help. I mean," he raised a shoulder, "she doesn't have to go to prison. But she has to see a psychologist and go on meds. I want a restraining order against her, too." He typed something into his phone. "Okay, they're adding that to the list."

"I hope she stays in jail." I stared at him with worried eyes.

"No, babe, she won't come after you." He reached for me, pulling me against his side. "You're with me now. I'll make sure she stays away from both of us."

They'd sentenced Genevieve to a psychiatric ward where she'd stay indefinitely. She was obsessed with Todd. They discovered a room dedicated to Todd; she had filled walls with pictures of him and me with a red 'X' drawn over my face. She threatened to kill us both if they ever released her. Her initial psych evaluation revealed many things, and the judge realized she needed help that a normal prison wouldn't give her.

"I'm so glad that's over," Todd said, pulling me onto his lap.

"So, six months have come and gone and you're still not sick of me," I said jokingly, wrapping my arm around his neck. Being this close to him I noticed he had a few strands of gray hair he didn't have before.

"Definitely not. We still have so much more exploring to do." He winked.

Todd's blood results had come back negative for anything nasty, but Genevieve became pregnant and had miscarried at the three-month mark. I could tell Todd had wanted a child, even though it was with someone like her. I was forty-five, already had my kids and didn't want more.

"Serious question," I started. "Do you want kids?"

He flinched as if I'd slapped him, and quickly glanced away before looking at me again. He shifted in his seat so that we could look at each other comfortably.

"I know where this is coming from," he said. "If I wanted a child I would've come to you so we could discuss it. I know you don't want more children—"

"Are you sure you still want to be with me? There are younger girls out there who can have children."

"What did I say about interrupting me?" he said, smacking my ass hard, then he kissed me. "Like I was saying," he grinned. "I honestly can't afford to have a child now, and there are too many things I still want to. And one of those things is to build a life with you for as long as possible. Okay? Okay. So it's settled then." He slapped my bum gently.

I hugged him tightly against me and kissed him.

"Now, what are we doing tonight, spreader bars or fuck swing?"

I squirmed. "The swing!"

About the Author

Blaire Little *is a lover of words, and has a sensual way of putting them together for your enjoyment. She hopes you enjoyed this book of little stories, and that you'll join her on her next adventure. Follow her on Amazon for the next release... or follow her on X (Twitter).*

𝕏

Printed in Great Britain
by Amazon